DATE DUE

			OR
DE' 0 4 02			
FE 0 4 08			
FE 1 5 08			
OR 1 1 08			
AP 1 1 08			
MY 1 7 08			
JE 2 5 08			
OC 0 5 09			
	WITHDRAWN		

THE WHOOP-UP TRAIL

**Center Point
Large Print**

**This Large Print Book carries the
Seal of Approval of N.A.V.H.**

THE WHOOP-UP TRAIL

B. M. BOWER

CENTER POINT PUBLISHING
THORNDIKE, MAINE

100807

This Center Point Large Print edition
is published in the year 2004 by arrangement with
Golden West Literary Agency.

Copyright © 1933 by B. M. Bower.
Copyright © renewed 1992 by Dele Newman Doke.

The text of this Large Print edition is unabridged. In other
aspects, this book may vary from the original edition. Printed in
Thailand. Set in 16-point Times New Roman type.

ISBN 1-58547-482-7

Library of Congress Cataloging-in-Publication Data

Bower, B. M., 1874-1940.
   The Whoop-up Trail / B. M. Bower.--Center Point large print ed.
      p. cm.
   ISBN 1-58547-482-7 (lib. bdg. : alk. paper)
    1. Large type books. I. Title.

PS3503.O8193W48 2004
813'.52--dc22

                                                        2004004695

Foreword

WHAT YEAR THE BUNCH GRASS FIRST WAS CRUSHED WHEN wild marching hoofs marked the trail that was to be, no man living may know. Years and years ago the great buffalo herds walked that way. Heads low and swinging with their stride, shaggy humps swaying a little too, head to tail they marched on those mysterious migrations up and down the plains. Always the same tracks to follow; the deep, wide trail where the bulls led the way and the cows followed meekly behind them; beside that trench a narrow, shallower one, where the calves walked alongside their mothers. Dozens of trails went in pairs like that; big deep ones for the grown-ups, little narrow trails for the young ones. Mile upon mile, up hills and down into hollows. Straight across the high level benches, dipping into creek bottoms and coulees, stopping short at a river bank where, if the herd must swim, mother buffaloes forced their calves to swim on the upstream side and watched against lagging; beginning again on the opposite shore. On and on, as far as the bunch grass grew and offered sweet grazing.

Indians followed those deep-worn buffalo trails. Braves on their painted ponies driving their horse herds before them. Squaws on shaggy camp ponies, loaded *travoix* behind. Papooses playing buffalo, walking the little calf trails.

After them, the traders, the trappers, the anxious emigrants—adventurers all.

And then the "bull trains" of yoked oxen, walking

head to tail as had the buffalo, but with never a moment of freedom; straining up the long slopes, walking with bent and swaying heads across the level benches, hauling long strings of heavy wagons loaded with freight for distant mining camp, trading post, fort. Dust and the popping of long-lashed, biting bull whips of rawhide; curses and clamor, and then silence and the twitter of birds, the chatter of prairie dogs popping out of their holes again to sit on their stubby tails and scold after the bull train had passed.

With the creaking, sweating bull trains, came the great slow herds of cattle, urged north by the tanned riders seeking new range, good water, untrodden miles of bunch grass where the buffalo once fed.

So, where the buffalo had pointed the way, there grew at last the old Whoop-up Trail.

Contents

1. One Rides Alone

A BULL TRAIN THAT HAD LEFT CAMP ON LITTLE PORCU-
pine Creek at dawn, by noon was creeping across the
benchland toward the Musselshell. Miles behind it a
ten-mule freight outfit was kicking up a cloud of dust
along the west end of Piney Buttes. Behind that, a ten-
mile stretch of empty prairie.

Then a rider appeared, coming up out of a grassy
hollow: A smooth-faced young fellow, a young cowboy
by the look of him, with a sensitive, curved mouth
drooping a little at the corners with weariness or
trouble—perhaps a combination of both. Big hat pulled
low over dark eyebrows shaded his eyes which looked
brown in the shadow, though one might easily expect
them to have tawny glints in sunlight. The youth of him
seemed hardened somehow, matured beyond his years;
the kind of maturity that went with the holstered gun
and the full-cartridged belt loosely buckled about his
flat slim body.

After him walked a small string of led horses; one
with a pack, led behind the saddle horse; a chestnut
mare with silvery mane and tail, a colt alongside that
would look like his mother in a year or two, and a yearling nipping grass off to one side of the trail and then
galloping madly to catch up again, silver mane tossing
in the breeze, glossy bay coat a-glisten.

Looking back over his shoulder to make sure the
truant gelding was not straying too far, the young
fellow's face brightened a little. Pride was in his glance,

9

together with a fond solicitude. But he yelled as if he meant nothing good for the yearling. "*You—Rummy!* What're you doing away back there? You get up here where you belong, before I brain you with a rock!" Then he whistled shrilly through his teeth.

The silver-maned mare sidled and half-turned, adding her remonstrating whinny to their master's command. It was exactly as if she cried, "You heard him, didn't you? Then you'd better get yourself up here in a hurry, if you know what's good for you!"

The young man grinned, looking at the mare. "That's the talk, Silvia. Read the riot act to him—if you don't, I sure will; come to a settlement, I'll have to put him on a lead rope or he'll get picked up."

Rummy couldn't have heard the threat, though he acted as though he had. With a loud "wait-for-me" whinny he came tearing up like a desert dust devil, passed the group with a derisive lift of his rump as he went by, and circled them, trotting with a high-kneed effortless stride which brought a shine to the young man's eyes as he watched.

But he wouldn't reveal his pride. "Think you're smart, don't you? If that's the way you feel about it, I'll slap a pack on you tomorrow and give old Jeff a rest." An empty threat not meant to be taken seriously even by Rummy.

Just then the long-legged colt, red now but called Silver because he would have the same creamy mane and tail as his mother, once he had shed his baby hair, created a diversion that left the gelding in peace for a while. Little red Silver decided that he was hungry and that the procession would have to halt until he had dined. His method was simple and effective. He merely trotted ahead of Silvia and crowded in against her front legs so she could not walk.

Silvia stepped aside, nipping him on the rump, but the colt lifted his heels to his mother, caught one over the lead rope and fell down. For that he was scolded, lifted by his young master and set upon his four bandy legs, spanked for punishment and permitted to gain his point.

Far down the trail to the south a loose ball of dust came rolling up across the prairie. The young man watched it while he loosened the cinch of his saddle and let his horse graze, bridle reins dropped to the ground. He rolled a cigarette, keeping one eye cocked toward the approaching dust; horsemen or a light rig, he knew by the speed they were making. When his cigarette was going, he called Rummy to him, coaxing with a lump of cut-loaf sugar held on his outstretched palm. The colt came trotting with the free springy stride it was a delight to watch. When his velvety upper lip quivered over the lump, the boy grinned and snapped a lead rope into the halter ring.

"Told you I would, didn't I?" he murmured caressingly. "If I let you have your way all the time, we never would get anywhere. You'd be gadding off after everybody that comes along. Now you'll behave yourself, maybe. You stand right here till your baby brother gets his dinner."

Rummy begged another lump of sugar and got it before his master tied him to the pack horse. Then Silvia must have a lump, and the saddle horse, Mike.

Old Jeff, the pack horse, was dozing with his eyes shut. He didn't like sugar, anyway. The baby was suckling avidly, fore-legs spraddled, bushy red tail swinging like a pendulum running away with itself.

Through the dust down the road the tossing heads of two dark horses emerged, a black, square shape swaying behind them. A light rig of some sort with canopy top. As it drew near, the young fellow stood with an arm flung over the neck of his horse Mike, smoking and smoothing tangles from Mike's mane, studiously incurious concerning his fellow travelers.

Nevertheless a quick sidelong glance or two gave him a fair knowledge of all surface details. Bay team, well kept but sweating now from the pace they must keep. A two-seated buggy. Three men crowded into the front seat; hard-eyed Westerners wearing town clothes and big range hats and guns. In the back seat a fat woman and a girl with light yellow hair banged and curling around her face.

The boy dared a third long look at the girl, because she leaned and looked down, smiling delightedly at little Silver getting his dinner. Even after the bay team had carried her past, the girl still leaned and looked back, watching the colt. The boy watched her from under his big hatbrim, and his eyes said he thought her beautiful. Which she was. But it might have been more to his advantage to observe how the three men eyed him and his outfit as they went by.

Then they were gone into the dust cloud again. Presently even that token of their passing had rolled down into a hollow out of sight. What dust hung above the trail settled into it and the land lay empty again, save for the boy and his little family of horses. When the colt had finished his refreshment and turned to dainty nosings along the trail, the young man tightened the cinch and swung into the saddle again. The leisurely journey continued, the boy staring out ahead as if impatient to reach the far skyline. Perhaps to follow the yellow-haired girl. But he would not hurry the baby of the family, and kept to the steady walk which he had wisely made his trail pace.

It was with some surprise that he rode down into the depression that had swallowed the fast trotting team and found the rig halted where the road swung around a bend and went twisting off along a straight-banked little stream. One glance told what had happened. The driver had been in too great a hurry coming down into this swale. One wheel had chugged violently into a deep rut and had splintered half its spokes. The fat woman was sitting on the bank, fanning herself with her bonnet, though the day was only pleasantly warm. The three men were nowhere in sight, nor was the girl. But from a cottonwood grove farther down the wash he heard the sound of chopping and guessed the men were after a pole to sling under the axle and hold the load fairly level until they reached some place where a new wheel could be had, or the broken one mended.

The boy had been taught nice manners. He lifted his big hat off his forehead. "Is there anything I can do to help?"

"No-o, I guess not." The woman looked at him, took a breath of decision and amended her answer. "You can tell Julie to come right back here to me. I can't have her straying off by herself like a hen turkey hunting grasshoppers. Picking flowers—to wilt in her hand and be thrown away again. You tell her I said to come right back here and quit stramming around alone."

The shyness of the boy showed in the darkening flush on his tanned face. "Yes, ma'am, I'll tell her." He rode on with his heart thumping. Her name was Julie, and like it or not, he had to speak to her when he found her. He had made a promise and promises had to be kept.

It was the barking of a small dog that told him where she was. Around three sharp turns in the road, completely out of sight and hearing of her companions. The boy frowned in disapproval of the girl's temerity. Her mother was right. It wasn't safe for a girl to wander around like that alone in this rough country. Even if she did have a dog—

Shucks. A little geezer about the size of your two fists. But it had a bark as shrill as a steam whistle. Evidently it had something cornered and was trying to scare it to death. As the boy rode up, he saw what it was even before his horses snorted and shied off. The girl was standing on a low flat rock embedded in the soil. Her hat was off and she was waving it frantically at the tiny dog, scolding and pleading. "Tiny, come here. Down, Sir. It'll *bite* you, Tiny. Here! Tiny!" A perfectly futile performance; just like a girl would act in a case like this, his face told eloquently his thought.

"Excuse me, miss," he said, dismounting at a safe distance where the horses would stand quiet and the colt would not wander too near. "If you'll come back over this way, I'll kill it."

She whirled and stared at him, startled for the moment. Then her glance returned to the snake. A big rattler, coiled and buzzing with rage, was watching its chance to strike. As the young fellow walked up, the snake launched itself forward, missing the dog by inches. Instantly it whipped into a coil again, its wicked triangular head flattened, eyes gleaming with a cold ferocity calculated to strike terror into anything living.

The little dog danced and circled, crouched and yapped as only small dogs can do until the boy picked up a pebble and threw it at the dog. His aim was accurate. The animal gave a yelp of astonishment, rolled over twice—fortunately not within reach of the snake—and got up, looking bewildered. Before he could return to his noisy quarrel with the snake, the boy had stepped in with his quirt. As the rattler lifted its head to the new enemy, a sharp side blow of the quirt caught him behind his *ugly* head and sent him limp and stunned in the grass.

"Grab your feist out of the way," the boy commanded, and finished the snake with two or three hard blows. "He's got his gall, tackling a rattler the size of this one; or any size, far as that goes."

With that he turned shy again and reddened under her gaze. She was not the young girl he had thought her when she passed him on the road. At least, she was not a schoolgirl, even though she did wear her hair down in curls, tied with a ribbon at the back of her neck. In her early twenties, a more seasoned judge would have guessed, with the poise and assurance of a young woman well accustomed to admiration.

"I'm awfully obliged," she said. "Tiny's such a spunky little dog, he'd fight anything. But a rattlesnake—ugh! I really can't thank you enough for coming to the rescue." She was looking at him rather strangely, with an odd intentness. Her eyes were a pansy blue, big and shining, with wide pupils which added a starry brilliance. And she continued to stare at him.

"Your mother wants you to go back," the boy said stiffly. "She asked me to tell you."

"Oh." The young woman frowned, cuddling the dog against her face. "She isn't my mother. I haven't any. She's my Uncle Barr's wife." She shrugged her slim shoulders and stepped down from the rock, holding her blue skirt in daintily at the side. She was such a little thing, once she was down on a level with the boy. She looked almost childlike.

Tall, stiff-necked from embarrassment, ears and neck flaming red, the young fellow looked down at her soberly. "You'd better go back, just the same," he said. "This is a pretty wild country; wild and tough, they tell me. You better stay with your folks." With that he touched his hat again, turned and walked over to his horses.

"Ever so much obliged," she called after him with a faint resentment in her voice, as if she were not used to seeing a man—even one so young—turn and walk away from her.

"Don't mention it," he replied with stereotyped politeness, speaking over his shoulder while he pre-

16

tended to be busy with the pack lashing.

She did not mention anything again; or if she did, her voice did not reach him, and his ears were keen. He waited, recinching his saddle to mark time until she was gone. When she had passed beyond the first bend, walking back toward the woman who was merely her uncle's wife, the boy did a thoroughly boyish thing. He went back to where the snake still feebly wriggled and pinched off the rattles for a keepsake.

He stood for a full minute staring at the flat rock where she had stood cuddling the dog Tiny against her cheek and staring at him with those blue and shining eyes. Even the memory of it brought the blood to his face again. He pulled out a white handkerchief, dingy from many creek washings but clean as soap and cold water could make it, and wiped his face carefully, looking at the cloth for smudges. There were none. A little dust, but not enough to make any woman stare.

So it wasn't that. His eyes grew puzzled. He stuffed the handkerchief into his pocket, returned to his patiently dozing horses and mounted, reining back into the trail.

Half a mile farther on his mouth relaxed into an absent smile which made him look younger and lonelier than he really was. "Julie," he pronounced under his breath. "Julie Barr."

2. Trouble on the Trail

THE LONG JUNE DAY GREW LANGUOROUS AS THE SUN slid toward the western line of hills. Twice the colt had stopped its mother, wanting to be fed. During the first halt the boy was covered with blushes because the crippled buggy passed him again and the young woman laughed and pointed, making the fat woman who was her uncle's wife stare. He was at that age which resents laughter more than hate. He vented his anger upon little Silver. "All you think of is stuffing your belly with milk! Gosh, she must think that's all I've got to do—stand around and watch you suck!"

But straightway he was staring after the dust cloud with another thought in his mind. He wished now that he had gone down into the cottonwood grove where the men had been chopping a pole for the broken buggy. Maybe one of them could have answered the question he had asked so many times all up the trail from Denver. Too late now. In spite of the dragging pole, they were making better time than he could without wearing out the colt. He wouldn't do that. In the three weeks and more they had spent on the trail, the little devil had grown like a pig. Stunt him now, and he never would amount to anything. They'd have to take it easy. No telling how much farther they'd have to travel.

The Whoop-up Trail. Sure was a lot of it. Not all of it the Whoop-up, though. There was all that stretch of country up through Colorado to Laramie, Wyoming. He had killed a lot of time around there, asking his question from ranch to ranch. Then on up through Wyoming following a will-o'-the-wisp of vague answers that finally petered out to nothing at all.

And then the word he had got at Lost Cabin. "You foller the Whoop-up Trail north from Billings, Bub. You inquire along up in there. Feller of that name went up with a herd of horses 'bout a year ago. Chances is he stayed up there. Lots uh the boys do. If he come back down into this country, I ain't heerd of 'im, and I'd be liable to." That was the old fellow who ran a store and post-office. He'd know, of course.

That was nearly three weeks ago. It wasn't much to go on, but it was a little better than nothing. A year is a long time for a man's name to linger in the memory of casual acquaintances, especially when men are drifting here and there through a wild and open country. The boy was too shy to mingle with the rough crowd around the saloons. Shy, and yet hard and cautious. He held aloof. And men gave him a curious glance or two as they passed by, thought he was with some one else and forgot about him. So those who might have answered his question never heard him ask it. And he rode on.

All that afternoon he watched the cloud of Julie's passing but he did not overtake it. Far behind him rose a slow-moving cloud that hung over the trail until nearly dusk. Cattle trailing up to the northern ranges. The boy urged his horses along a little faster. There was not much danger that the trail herd would come up with him, but he would just as soon put more distance between them. Not that he feared the cowboys—he rather liked the bold riders of the free ranges; but he did not want Rummy fooling around strange horses. He might get kicked or something, he was such a sassy, chancey little devil. The colt too. Just as well to keep off by himself.

Yet that night he camped in a grassy creek bottom no more than a long stone's throw from a freight outfit just pulled in from the north. That was different. The mules were in the care of a herder and were grazing nearly a mile down the creek where the grass was not eaten off. His own horses he hobbled and turned loose above his camp where he could watch them. They would not go far from the little tepee tent he set up beside his camp fire in case a storm blew up in the night. No sign of it now, but one never could tell, this time of year.

The other fire looked friendly, shining through the dusk. Two men pottered around the wagons, then settled down beside the fire to lounge and smoke before they turned in. The boy sized them up, turned and cast a comprehensive glance around his own outfit, saw that Rummy and the colt were lying down, and strolled over to the mule-skinners' fire.

"Evenin', Bub," the older of the two called out cheerfully as he came up. The other, a small sandy man with squinty blue eyes, nodded over the pipe he was filling.

"Good evening, sir. Nice weather we're having for traveling."

The mule-skinner stroked his long drooping mustache down each side of his mouth with a practiced double swipe of his left thumb. The young fellow's sharp eyes detected the grin that was being hidden behind the movement and he flushed, hating to be laughed at when he didn't know why.

"Liable to have a storm, though, any time now. Set down. Kinda lonesome travelin' alone, ain't it?"

"Yes—but my horses are lots of company."

"Them's two fine colts you got there," the sandy man spoke up. "Jim and me was just talking about 'em."

"Their mother's got fine blood in her," the boy stated proudly. "The yearling was sired by a running horse. He's a streak of lightning right now, when he gets strung out, the colt is going to be a dandy too."

"Yeah, we was noticin' them colts when you rode in. Goin' fur?" A touchy question in that day and country, but the old fellow made it sound very casual.

"Well, I don't know. I hope not much farther." The boy hesitated before putting the question he had asked so often along the trail. "I'm looking for Wane Bennett. Do you happen to know him—or anything about him?"

"Wane—Bennett?" The old fellow took his pipe from his mouth, cuddled it in his hand. "You wouldn't mean old Graveyard Bennett, I don't s'pose?"

"Not if he's old, I wouldn't. Wane's twenty-three; be twenty-four next October. He—"

"'Taint Graveyard, then. He's a man old as I be or older—and I was foaled more'n fifty years ago. Young squirt, hunh? Friend of yourn?"

"My brother. The only one I've got. The only relative, so far as I know."

"Kinda wondered why a young one like you was hittin' the trail alone. Lookin' for your brother, hunh?"

The boy hunkered down on his rider's boot heels and got out papers and tobacco. He nodded, singling out a

21

leaf and tearing it from the book. He snapped the rubber band around the book, slipped it back into his shirt pocket, tore a tiny strip carefully from the paper and rolled it into a hard little ball between thumb and finger. He snapped that in to the fire and proceeded to roll a cigarette with the narrowed piece of paper.

The mule-skinner chuckled. "I mind a feller up at Cow Island 'bout a year ago went through all that p'formance to git himself a smoke. Stingy with paper. Only one I ever seen, till now."

"I like to taste the tobacco when I smoke. I hate these saddle blankets they hand out for cigarette papers." He ran his tongue tip along the paper edge, looking at the other. "Maybe that was my brother you saw. I guess I got the habit from Wane when I started smoking."

"Mighta been, son. Stranger t' me. I jest happened to be standin' facin' him at the bar. He let a drink wait while he monkeyed around strippin' a cigarette paper down t' suit 'im. 'Bout your size—only filled out more. 'Bout your style, near as I remember. Wouldn't 'a' thought a word about 'im, only fer that glass uh beer goin' flat, waitin' on 'im. Looked funny."

"I'll bet that was Wane. Cow Island, you say? That's where the ferry is, isn't it?"

"That's her."

Squinty injected a sentence. "I mind that feller. John, that was the time them hoss thieves was rounded up—"

"Long about then," John agreed. "Fur's that goes, they're always roundin' up hoss thieves. You want to look out, Bub, and don't go throwin' in with any Tom,

Dick, er Harry that comes along. Liable t' find yerself in scaly comp'ny."

"That," said the young fellow grimly, "is what I've been doing; looking out. Nobody's bothered me so far. If they did, I'd sure try and look out for myself and my horses. I don't pack a gun just for an ornament."

"I bet yo're a hard customer," the mule-skinner agreed, wiping down another grin. "Where's yore private graveyard, kid?"

The boy flushed and got to his feet with one limber lift of his body. "So far," he said stiffly, "I've managed to avoid any digging. I just drag 'em off where they won't stink. Good night."

As he stalked off to his own camp, he heard the older man curse. "Dammit, Squint, I wish't you'd keep yore big mouth shut. If I hadn't of headed yuh off there—"

The boy walked on out of hearing, wondering a little why Squint had needed to be headed off. It couldn't have been anything about Wane, for they didn't know him; they said so. What made him hot was that patronizing way some folks had of treating him like a kid. Joshing him about private graveyards, just because he packed a gun. Hunh! He'd be a fool to start out on the trail without one, and they knew it.

Early as the freighters made ready to leave next morning, the Bennett boy was earlier. They shouted a friendly, "So long, Bub—be good t' yourself," and he waved his hand for answer, much as he hated being called "Bub." Eighteen wasn't so darned young. Just because he didn't wear whiskers down to his belt buckle, was no sign he couldn't take a man's place in

23

the world. Unconsciously he stroked his brown cheeks and chin, hoping for a roughness and feeling only a silky fuzz on upper lip and chin. That night he'd shave, anyway. It was that fuzz made him look so darned silly and young. Gave folks a wrong impression.

As a matter of fact, it did. And that day his manner repelled any idea of such familiarities as he had suffered the night before. The trouble was, he did not meet any one within speaking distance. A bull train creeping down the trail while he was making a noon camp well out away from passers-by; three horsemen riding in a hurry, blanket rolls and slickers tied behind their cantles; a six-horse freight team hauling three wagons, going north. And away to the south, the broad blanket of dust where the trail herd plodded steadily northward.

That day he traveled, and half of the next, pulled forward by the hope that at the Missouri crossing he would hear some definite word of Wane. Drawn also by the occasional gouged mark in the trail, showing where the buggy with the broken wheel had limped along to the river. Again his moody lips half smiled when he thought that Julie might be at Cow Island crossing, held there while they mended that wheel.

His first glimpse of the big river thrilled him as he rode down out of the breaks and saw it, a broad silver band sliding along in the distance. Then he was down in a wide willow flat, winding in and out, seeing nothing of river or town for a mile or more. He did see a brace of grouse and shot the head neatly off the cock, firing from the saddle without seeming to take any careful aim at all; a performance that might have interested the old freighter had he seen it.

At the first open glade where a little creek ran down among the willows to the river, he turned aside and made camp, unpacking only what he needed for supper. The colts needed rest and he had a youthful instinct to fill up before he went among strangers. So he cleaned and cooked the grouse, frying it in bacon grease. With cold bannock and hot black coffee he feasted royally and lay back afterward for a smoke before he went on.

With Rummy safely necked to steady old Jeff, and with little Silver poddy and satisfied, after having dined at leisure, he returned to the trail and made his way along the brush-bordered road to the settlement. At a glance he saw that it could not be called a town, nor even a village. A rambling log building that seemed to be a combination of saloon, hotel and trading post stood back against a young cottonwood grove, and across the road from it stood a blacksmith shop, a wagon yard and stable. Down next the river the squat ferry barge lay snubbed to the great cable that sagged swaying across the wide river, the ferryman's cabin back up on the bank, out of the way of spring freshets.

For the rest, trampled sandy earth, refuse of countless camp fires on the flat he was crossing, and a wing of fence to hold the herds from scattering down the bank, away from the ford. The broad sweep of current made it look dangerous for swimming.

The sun was just setting, laying a path of molten gold across the water. A last bar of sunlight struck coppery glints from Silvia's neck and shoulder, where she stood alongside Jeff at the long hitch rail before the store, her colt reaching up to touch her soft nose. At another rail before the saloon steps two thin-flanked saddle horses stood dozing, their coats roughened from hard riding. With a comprehensive glance around him that saw and stored up small details which most men would have passed over, he went into the store.

Ten minutes or so later he emerged with a gunny sack comfortably heavy with packages. He had not asked his question of the clerk who was alone in the store, because the fellow said at once that he had just come from the East and hated the place and meant to go back as soon as he had money enough. No use asking a man of his type; he wouldn't know anything about anybody.

Two men were standing by the hitch rail eyeing Silvia and the two colts. As he came down the steps, carrying his sack of purchases, they turned and watched him without a word. With a turn or two of the saddle strings hanging at the side of his cantle he fastened the sack, took a couple of half hitches and turned to untie the lead ropes. His glance went sidelong to the men, expecting to read admiration, perhaps a little envy in their faces; they weren't the first to cast covetous eyes on that trio, and he was all ready to grin and say nope, they weren't for sale at any price.

But they weren't looking at the horses, they were looking at him. And one of the men had a hand on his gun. With the other he tilted his coat lapel so that metal blinked in the sunlight. It looked like a star.

"Just a minute, young feller. These your horses?"

"They most certainly are. For the time being, anyhow."

"And what might that mean?"

"Well, it means that my brother owns the mare and the yearling, and I'm taking them to him. The colt's mine. I get half the increase for taking care of 'em. The other two horses I own."

"Hm-mm. And what might your name be?"

"It might be most anything, but it happens to be Claude Bennett, if that's any of your business."

"It shore is my business. Where you from?"

"Denver, Colorado. I was born and raised near there."

"Long ways from home, ain't you?" Against the sun glare the man half closed his eyes and moved a step to one side. "Where'd you get them horses?"

Claude Bennett looked at him, drew an angry breath, caught the gleam of metal again and sighed. "The saddle horse and pack horse I bought. I can show the bill-of-sales for them. As I told you, the mare and yearling belong to my brother. The colt is mine for taking care of the rest."

"Got the papers for that?"

"No." A gleam of suspicion came into his keen eyes. "I wasn't dealing with folks like you. Anything my brother said he'd do is good as forty papers. I expect my brother has something to show, but I'm not sure. Dad gave Silvia to him when she was a colt."

"Hm-mm. What put you on the road?" The man's gaze traveled slowly over the outfit. "Kinda young to be goin' it alone."

"Young in years, mebbe, but old in cussedness," his companion muttered.

"What you doin' here? Quit lyin' and tell it straight.

27

Why ain't you home where you belong?"

The boy caught his breath, but his eyes were steady. "I haven't a home any more. I was living with my mother. She died. She told me to find Wane and stay with him."

"Wane? Who's he?"

"Wane Bennett's my brother. I told you I'm looking for him. I thought maybe I'd find him—around here somewhere." His eyes turned toward the building and a flash came into them as his glance steadied upon a certain window. He could have sworn that he saw Julie looking out at him. Moreover, he had a swift impression of her scared, anxious eyes as she glanced from him to the two men. The tall man with the badge turned and looked, but the face was gone. The shorter man was still staring at the mare and colt.

"Something damn' scaly about that reversed EB," he said. "Take a look, Dave. That brand's been worked over. I know that mare."

"You sure are quick to get acquainted with, old-timer," the boy retorted. "Unless you saw her down around Denver, you never laid eyes on her till I rode up a few minutes ago."

"Didn't, ay? That's an LP mare; belongs to a friend uh mine back up the Musselshell. Reverse LP. Skin her and I'll prove it. Her old brand'll show up on the inside uh the hide."

The boy, Claude Bennett, looked from him to Silvia. Tight little lines pulled in the corners of his mouth. "You'll have to skin me first, then," he gritted, and stepped to Silvia's side where the colt nudged him

28

unheeded. "No man lays a hand on my horses. Not while I'm alive, anyway."

"Not if you can prove they're yours, certainly not. All we aim to do is protect honest men around here and clean out the bad element that's tryin' to get a foothold." The tall man cleared his throat, glanced from Claude to the short man. "Shaner here claims he knows that mare: If he's mistaken, you'll have to prove it. We know how to deal with horse thieves around here," he added grimly.

"You certainly seem to know some new wrinkles about stealing horses," Young Bennett cried hotly. "You and your LP talk! I happen to know when my father put that EB on this mare. I was just a kid, but I was right there. It was five years ago, a few miles east of Denver. So I *know* you're lying when you say she belongs on the Musselshell."

"Careful how you talk, young feller," the tall man warned him harshly. "If you was honest and above-board, you wouldn't get so hot under the collar when you're asked a few questions. I think," he said briskly, "you'll bear investigatin'. You take charge of the outfit, Shaner. I'll just lock this feller up till we can set on his case. Hand over your gun, you—"

"You go to hell!"

But young Claude Bennett was no match for these two. There before the store, within sight of half a dozen windows, they tricked him. The tall man had the drop on him. The short man moved up, reaching for the mare's lead rope, and suddenly he jumped in and drove a vicious blow to the point of the boy's jaw. Young Ben-

29

nett dropped as if lightning had struck him.

3. "Everybody Calls Me Chip"

AN UNPLEASANT YET HALF-FAMILIAR SMELL PERVADED that uneasy cloudiness which held young Bennett poised between clear thinking and the black void of complete unconsciousness. An earthy odor mingled with something that bothered him, gave him the uncomfortable feeling that some hated task had to be done and that he was too tired or too sick to make a beginning upon it. After an indeterminate time he recognized the smell as sprouted, half-rotten potatoes. He thought it was his job to sprout potatoes; that is, to rub off the sprouts, as each spring he must do when he was a child on the ranch near Denver.

That accounted for the knobby lumps beneath him. He opened his eyes, looked upon blackness. Yet he knew that he was lying against a pile of old potatoes and guessed he was in a cellar somewhere. But a whisper of June wind touched his face fitfully, as if it must creep in to where he lay. And then, looking straight up to the roof, he saw where the breeze came from; a square ventilator cut into the roof not so very far above his head.

Now that he noticed it he could see a pale star floating in a greenish dark sky which he watched, knowing that it would be twilight outside. Now and then a branch tip swayed across his vision, blotting out the star. So by that he guessed that he was in a root cellar out somewhere behind the building. He had observed the grove of young cottonwoods back there, had marked their slender trunks and thin branches clothed with glossy young leaves. He had thought them beautiful.

Nothing was beautiful now. It was when he attempted to lift an exploring hand to his swollen, aching jaw that he remembered exactly what had happened and why he was lying on a malodorous heap of old potatoes in a root cellar with his hands tied behind him. One decisive movement of his legs told him his feet were tied, and he was pretty sure his jaw was broken.

He wriggled and twisted, trying to work his hands free, but nothing was accomplished except some painful abrasions on his wrists and a position where he could no longer look up and see the star. That worried him until he had the square patch of sky, the star and the branch tip in full view again. Being able to see out made a difference. Things didn't seem quite so hopeless.

But things were bad enough. They were trying to make him out a horse thief. Getting keyed up to hang him, probably, so they could grab his horses without danger of being strung up for thieves themselves. He'd heard of frame-ups like this before. He had listened to men talk of gruesome happenings along the Whoop-up Trail, of innocent men accused and executed by masked men who called themselves Vigilantes. Like the days of Forty-nine in California, it had sounded to him, remote and legendary, with little foundation in fact. The Trail as he had traveled it had been long and lonesome. No place for masked riders—where men could ride mile after mile and never be seen, even though they rode in broad day-light.

But this was not remote, nor was it legendary. Incredible, yes. One of those unbelievable things that happen just when you are least prepared. But his tight bonds were actual facts, for they were making his hands big and wooden-feeling. The root cellar was real too; that old potato smell was stifling.

Young Bennett dug elbows into the pile and sat up, staring this way and that into the dark. Not a glimmer of light could he see, and now that he had moved, his star was gone. Half ashamed of the weakness, he lay back again, inching himself this way and that until it shone silvery in its little square patch of sky—not greenish now, but a deep purple. The star was brighter too, and when the branch tip swayed across, he could no longer distinguish the leaves, save as vague blots against the blue.

And then, although he did not move at all, the square went black. Only for a second or two, however. Then a subdued, anxious voice called down to him; a half whisper utterly strange to hear. "Are you there?"

A trick, perhaps. Young Bennett kept still.

"Young man—who killed the rattlesnake—with a quirt—are you down there?"

"Yes," young Bennett answered, and felt the jump of his heart, the racing blood as it rushed tingling through his veins.

"Oh. Are you—all right?"

A silly question to ask, but it did not sound silly to him then.

"I'm tied hand and foot—is all."

"Oh. What was it—for? What did you do?"

"Nothing. Just happened to have some good horses, I guess."

"Oh—*no!* They must have thought you—stole them."

"Well, I didn't." Had she been a man he would have sworn at her. "They belong to me—and my brother."

"Your *brother?*" An odd quaver gave the word a significance he must have felt.

He answered the tone. "I'm looking for my brother, Wane Bennett—"

"Wane!" Again her voice was shaken with some emotion.

"Yes. Do you know Wane? I'm his brother—"

"Not his little brother—*Chip?*" Then she wailed, "Oh! His brother—Chip!"

"Why? Sure, they—everybody always called me Chip. Where is Wane? You know him! Is he here?"

Suddenly he was looking at the star. Julie was gone. To bring Wane? But in as small a place as Cow Island Wane would have spotted the horses. He'd know Silvia as far as he could see her. He'd know what had happened and he'd be tearing the place apart to get his kid brother Chip. Why, Wane would—

She was back again. He saw the ventilator darkened when Julie's face bent over it. "Chip!"

"Yes? Where's Wane? Did you tell him?" But even as he spoke, he knew she couldn't have had time for that.

"No. I—Wane isn't here, Chip. I—I haven't seen him—for a long time." Her voice sounded strained and colorless, almost cold.

"You know him, though. Don't you? He's all right, isn't he?"

He waited for her answer. Then, "Yes—he's—all right, Chip." Her next words were hurried. "I've got to do something. I—I can't let them—" She was whispering now, talking to herself. "They *shan't!* Wane Bennett's kid brother—Chip! Oh, I—it's horrible! They mustn't do it—they—*can't!*"

"Can't you—if you could get in here and untie me. Could you do that, Julie?" It never occurred to him that he was bold to use her name like that. "I can hold my own—"

"Oh, no! I can't. I wouldn't dare! But don't give up, Chip. I think—I'll see what I can do."

The star again, and the swaying branch against the faint light. This time Julie did not come back.

Wane Bennett's kid brother Chip watched and waited and listened. The star slid farther and farther toward the edge, winked and was gone. Another star slipped up to peer down at him. A rat in a corner of the cellar startled him with its thumping scurry. He remembered ghastly tales of rats attacking helpless prisoners and he drew up his knees and kicked wilted potatoes toward that corner. He heard a scamper, then silence filled the dank place. A long sigh escaped him. He was ashamed of the way his heart was thumping, but he always had hated rats.

What horrible thing was it that they mustn't do to Wane's kid brother Chip? Hang him for a horse thief? He shut his eyes and tried to visualize what it would be like, but the picture blurred and broke under his incredulity. He wasn't a thief. If they looked in his war bag they'd find his bill-of-sales for Mike and Jeff, and he didn't claim to own Silvia and Rummy. Even if they wanted to frame him, they wouldn't dare to go the limit. Not right here at the ferry, where people were coming and going all the time, and there were women living right in the house. Not in broad daylight. Not to him, anyway. Good Lord, it *couldn't* happen.

His head ached with a splitting throb that seemed about to tear his skull open. His arm muscles cramped, and each potato beneath his body became a separate torment. And suddenly his imagination awoke to the fact that other men might have lain there in that cellar, telling themselves the worst couldn't happen to them. And it had happened. Julie's frantic worry proved that.

If she had dared come down and untie him he could have defended himself. He'd fight to the finish, and if he went out fighting—why, a fellow had to go some-time. But to lie here tied like an outlaw steer, waiting for them to show up—to take him out in the woods somewhere and *hang* him! Chip Bennett, hanged for a horse thief! Left to swing in the wind; left as a warning, for men to ride up and stare at while they rolled them-selves a smoke—

Lines of sweat ran down his cheeks, tasted salty in the corners of his tight-shut mouth that still held a boyish curve. But there were no tears. And when he caught himself panting under the spell of horror that gripped him, sturdy pride swept in to steady his young man-hood. A strain of the stoic in him came to the rescue and made him cool and calm, his lip curled with contempt for their vile hypocrisy.

Let them come. They wouldn't have the satisfaction of hearing him beg for mercy. There was no mercy in them or they would never do it. It would be murder, and he'd tell 'em so with his last breath. And he wouldn't want to be in their boots when Wane found out about it. Wane would sure make them wish they'd never been born. He'd shoot them down like dogs.

That thought somehow comforted him, eased the ache in his head and jaw. He was young and he had been in the saddle since sunrise. Thinking with gloomy relish of the terrible vengeance Wane would wreak upon his murderers, young Chip drifted off into a nightmarish sleep, his swollen jaw faintly lighted by the star.

4. Julie Makes a Bargain

SUPPER WAS NEARLY OVER AT THE LANG HOTEL. At dusk a hand-bell shaken vigorously on the front porch had clamored a summons which Chip Bennett, down in the root cellar behind the house, could not hear. Julie, waiting on the few diners, had spilled three little oblong dishes of canned corn, a platter of fried venison liver and a cup of coffee off the tray she was carrying into the dining room, and had her ears boxed by her obese aunt, who called her a name the meaning of which neither quite knew. Julie's deft fingers were all thumbs that evening and her aunt accused her of being rattle-pated—though that was not the name she had called her a few minutes before.

The tray had tilted when Shaner and Dave Burch, the tall man with the badge, came in and sat down at the table where Barr Lang, the proprietor, was already feeding his huge body with hot corn bread and venison, his elbows spread comfortably at the head of the long table. Julie caught the sidelong look her uncle gave the two as they pulled out their chairs and sat down. She tried to read his face, tried to guess how much he knew and whether he would tolerate the thing they meant to do. Her uncle was a good man—how fiercely she clung to that goodness of his!—always helping people, always ready to tell a funny story. Accommodating was the word most often applied to Barr Lang by his fellows.

But would he be accommodating enough to save a nice-looking boy accused of stealing horses? Julie thought perhaps if she went at him just right— Her Uncle Barr was jolly, full of jokes as a rule, but tonight he had no smile for her, no word. So far as his manner went, she might have been a squaw handing him his coffee. If she knew how to approach him—but she didn't. Though her hand brushed his sleeve, Barr Lang himself was as remote and as inaccessible to her as the moon.

Two freighters came in, ogled her with sly glances, nudged each other like schoolboys when she retreated to the kitchen. Barr Lang pushed back his chair with a harsh scraping sound, flicked Dave Burch and Shaner with a careless glance and went out, picking his teeth. Shaner and Burch tapped their cups with their tin teaspoons, signaling for more coffee. Throwing a bound young prisoner into an evil-smelling cellar and leaving him there to await their convenience did not seem to impair their appetites.

Julie brought coffee, more venison liver and steaks, refilled the plate with corn bread, carried out the freighters' empty cups and returned with them full. Her step was light and springy, her starched white apron, trimmed with lace she herself had crocheted, made a pleasant little whispery sound when she walked. But her cheeks were white and her eyes had a haunted look. Her small mouth was pale and tight and she would neither smile nor speak when the youngest freighter paid her a compliment and asked if she had baked that dried-apple pie.

But at last even the two freighters were filled to the chin and could find no further excuse for loitering there, but plucked their grimy hats from under their chairs and took themselves off. Julie stood with their stacked dishes in her two hands, listening in dread of what she might hear. There would be some pretense of a trial, she knew. But how soon? What the verdict would be even she did not need to guess. The horrible certainty of it was what froze her blood. Wane Bennett's kid brother Chip! No more a horse thief than she was, she thought fiercely, and dropped into her Uncle Barr's chair and beat her temples with her small fists as if that might beat some inspiration from her brain.

Steps came to the closed door, paused while the knob turned, and the door opened on its squeaky hinges. Julie gasped and stood up, stiff and straight and on guard. Then abruptly she relaxed. "Oh-h! It's you."

A tall young cowboy came in, spur chains clanking dully under his insteps, big rowels burring on the bare floor as he walked. His sunny blue eyes had an habitual twinkle. His wide humorous mouth wore a cheerful grin which nothing seemed able to quench for long. His big gray hat was off and dangling in his hand—and that it was his left hand held an unconscious significance to which neither gave a thought. It meant that even a tall lad who smiled at life as this one did might need his gun hand ready for instant action, and that the possibility had bred the habit of using the left for little things.

"Too late for supper, Miss Lang? Gee, I've been hitting the high spots to get here." Then his warm glance took a shade of concern and his voice dropped a note. "What's the matter? You're white as a sheet. Yuh sick? Aw gee!"

"No, but—Oh, Will, they've arrested Wane Bennett's brother for horse stealing! You knew—you remember Wane?"

"Sure I do. What's his brother doing here?"

"Oh, it's awful! He came here looking for Wane, and he brought some of Wane's horses. We passed him on the road, and he had a beautiful mare and two colts besides the pack horse. Chestnut sorrel, she was, with silver mane and tail, and the biggest colt was just like her. And Burch and Shaner—Shaner knocked him down and they carried him to—" her voice dropped to a horrified whisper—*"to the root cellar."*

The young cowboy shivered. "Good Lord! Then they must figure on—"

"Oh, they do! And he's just a boy. The kid brother, Chip, that Wane talked about. About your age, Will—and he looks so much like Wane it—it gave me the creeps almost. I went and talked to him down the ventilator and found out who he is, and—oh, he thinks W-wane will c-come and s-s-save—" Fight as she would, tears filled her voice so she could not go on.

With his teeth set hard together the cowboy swallowed. "Yuh know what time they figure on doing it?"

Julie shook her head, crowding a corner of her apron against her mouth to stifle her sobs. The cowboy, whose name, by the way, was Will Davidson, generally called Weary Willie for some obscure reason, reached out a shy hand and patted her elbow awkwardly, trying to give some comfort. "Now, don'tcha cry, Miss L—Julie. I don't know right now what we can do about it, but we sure got to do *something*. I'd go bawl Dave Burch out myself, if it'd do any good. For a long time now he's been getting too darn free with his rope. Making him captain of the Vigilantes has sure swelled his head worse'n a lump-jaw steer. Don't you worry. Wane Bennett's brother Chip is sure going to find plenty of backers in this country, you know that."

"Yes," Julie retorted fiercely, "after it's too late to do him any good!" Then she spoke more calmly. "If you had time to get Milt Cummings, maybe he could stop them. If I asked him—"

"Sure. Milt's in the barroom right now, Julie. We rode over together."

"Oh, why didn't you *say* so? Go get him quick! Tell him Julie Lang wants to see him right away! Hurry, Will! No telling what minute—"

"You bet!" Will Davidson wheeled and darted out, making surprisingly little noise about it, because he took long steps on his toes. Yet with all his hurry he did not go at once to the saloon. Once off the steps he walked quickly to the hitch rail and untied his horse, leading him past the saloon corner and dropping the reins to the ground in the shadow of the building. Barring a stampede past him, the horse would stand there all night, if necessary, and would be found in the morning in almost the identical spot where he had been left. Weary Willie had no anxiety on that score.

He retraced his steps to the barroom door, held the knob an instant while he listened. Then he opened the door and stepped in. Behind the bar stood Lang, leaning half over it as he talked in an undertone with Dave Burch and a big, handsome young man who was Milt Cummings, owner of the Lazy Ladder outfit across the river and Weary Willie's boss. A dozen feet away and facing the door, Shaner was sitting before a solitaire spread, holding a black ten-spot in his hand while he scanned the cards. Over against the side wall the two freighters were playing cribbage, a bottle and two small glasses convenient to their hands.

All very peaceful. Too peaceful to be genuine, Weary Willie decided. Lang looked up at him, breaking off in his speech. Dave Burch turned and glared over his shoulder. Milt also wore the indefinable air of intrusion.

Weary stopped just inside the door, his grin wide and unconcerned. "Say, Milt, that bronk of yours has got himself tangled up in the rope. You want to get him outa the mess, or shall I?"

"I'll come." Milt threw a glance at his two companions. "Back in a minute," Weary heard him mutter, as he started for the door.

Weary Willie backed out and waited for him on the porch. "Say, I lied to yuh, Milt," he confessed engagingly. "Your cayuse is all right. Julie Lang wants to see you right away. I kinda thought maybe I better not holler it right out, in there."

"Damn right. Thanks, Weary." Milt stepped off on to the ground and hurried off toward the dining room.

Weary cast one long look after him and ducked around the corner, picking up the reins of his horse as he passed and leading him on into the edge of the grove. It was quite dark back there already, and a rising wind rustled in the branches, covering what little sound they made.

Back in the dining room Julie was talking urgently in a nervous undertone while she pretended to arrange a place for Milt Cummings at the table. "I'll bring you coffee and things—Aunt Amanda might come in if she hears us talking and you aren't eating—" And she hurried out with her big, black tray.

Out behind the house, on the bank at the edge of the grove, Weary Willie was lying on his belly with his face pressed close to the ventilator top. "Hey! H' are yuh, down there?"

And from below Chip's voice answered with suppressed eagerness, "That you, Wane?"

"No—it's nobody you know. Say, how yuh fixed? Tied up I s'pose?" Away from Julie, his words were clipped and careless. His voice, too, had lost some of its easy drawl.

"Tied tight as a drum. Why?"

"Well, I was just wondering. If I was to drop a rope down in there, d' you s'pose you could get the loop down over your shoulders?"

"Might, if you could drop the loop over my head—and didn't take in the slack too soon!"

"Fine and dandy. Wait till I do some work on this damn roof. Better shut your eyes, old-timer, if you don't want 'em full up with dirt."

"Say," Chip called guardedly, "aren't you taking a pretty big risk?"

And Weary Willie, even in that tense moment, chuckled. "Shucks! Life would be plumb weary without risks in it. Look out below! Liable to be a ton er two uh dirt land on yuh in a minute here."

In the dining room, Milt Cummings was stirring three spoons of sugar slowly into his coffee, a corner of his lip caught in between his teeth. The hanging lamp over the table brought a reddish cast into his brown hair and revealed the wave which no amount of combing could flatten permanently.

He looked up at Julie standing with both hands on the table across from him, the light full on her corn-yellow hair and her white strained face. Shadowed by her long lashes, her eyes looked almost black. Milt's eyes, turned toward the lamp, were a greenish gray with almost an emerald glint between his half-shut lids. "Sure it's because he's just a kid?" He leaned toward her, watching her face. "Sure it ain't Wane you're thinking of?"

"Oh, no! No! But he's just a boy, Milt! And he saved my Tiny from a big rattlesnake the other day. We passed

43

him on the road, and when we broke a wheel he over-took us. I was picking flowers and a snake was fighting Tiny, and he came along and killed it. He's just a shy, bashful boy, Milt, and he *couldn't* be a horse thief."

"Boys ain't always so bashful with horses," Milt murmured, glancing down at his plate. "Uh course, saving that sample of a dog for you—I can see how you might feel kinda under obligations to him. But he could save a real man-size dog and still be a horse thief. Girls get funny notions sometimes," he added, with a sigh and a faint negative movement of his head. But all the while he was watching Julie from under his straight dark brows.

She beat a fist softly on the table. "Milt, you must! If you'll save him, Milt, I—I'll do *anything!*" A tinge of red crept into her cheeks. "Anything, Milt." And her eyes dropped away from his gaze.

"Anything, hunh?" Milt slowly laid the spoon down in his saucer. "Does that mean—you'll marry me, Julie?"

"Oh, yes! Yes, I'll marry you. Only you must save him from Dave Burch and—" Her voice broke on the words.

Milt got up slowly, went around the table and dropped his hands on her shoulders, turning her to face him.

Julie gasped. "Oh, Milt—the windows—some one might look in—"

Milt frowned and let her go. "You aren't just playing me for a sucker, are you?"

"No, I'll be grateful enough to—marry you, Milt, if

you'll stop those awful Vigilantes from—h-hanging that poor boy. I—"

"Just grateful, Julie? That the best you can do?" Milt stood close, looking down on the top of her head.

"I—I guess not," whispered Julie, and gave him a quick upward glance. "You'll have to hurry. After-wards—"

"Afterwards, I'll be back in the grove. Waiting."

Julie pleated the red tablecloth in tiny folds. "Aunt Amanda watches me like a hawk," she whispered, "but I'll try to come—for just a minute."

Milt dipped thumb and fingers into a vest pocket and pulled out a tiny buckskin bag. In complete silence he unfastened it, held it open so that she must look. "I've been packin' that ring for over a year, Julie," he said in a hushed tone. "Ever since you took it off—on Wane Bennett's account. Now, by God—"

"It wasn't—on Wane's account. You—you'd no right to accuse me without—"

"I guess," said Milt, in that same repressed tone, "we better not dig up that old argument again. It never did get us anywhere, girlie. But if that ring goes on your finger again, it better not come off again or I—"

Julie straightened, threw back her head. "Do you want to kill time here until it's too late, just because he's Wane Bennett's brother?"

"No. That sure ain't any gilt-edged recommendation, coming from you. But I'll do what I can. I might not be able to talk Dave over. What then?"

"I made my bargain," Julie said, and pinched her mouth in stubbornly. "You save that boy, and I'll marry you. I guess," she added pertly, "if you want me bad enough, you'll find some way to get around Dave. But if you fool around all night just *talking*—"

From the kitchen a voice rose shrewishly. "Jul*ee*! Have them dirty dishes growed fast to the table in there? You get 'em out here and be quick about it!"

"When you hear an owl hoot three times back in the grove—you better find some way of getting out there," Milt said hastily, and went off without drinking the coffee he had so painstakingly sweetened.

Julie was already clattering dishes upon the tray. She nodded, but her mouth still had that pinched, stubborn look.

5. Weary Takes a Hand

WILL DAVIDSON SAT BACK ON HIS BOOT HEELS, PUSHED his big hat off his forehead and stared at the dark bulk of the building no more than a hundred feet away. Lamplight shone through the back windows of the saloon—which the Lang family always referred to as the barroom. But the two windows were set high in the log wall and a man would have to walk in behind the bar and lean over a stack of beer kegs to look out of the handiest one, and if he took all that trouble he couldn't see anything, anyway. Weary Willie had that all figured out in his mind and the windows did not concern him at all.

What did worry him was the probability that Dave Burch or Shaner would come to the cellar. It was a risk that drew beads of dampness on his forehead, but sitting there waiting for them to come merely asked for trouble. He had been longer than he had expected to be already. That roof had certainly been built for a hard winter. They'd find use for two ropes instead of one, if they came and caught him there, and no ifs or ands about it. So the sooner he finished the job the better.

None of his worry crept into his cautious whisper, however. He leaned and thrust his face into the hole he had made by lifting three pole ends aside. "How yuh fixed now? Can you set up right here under me?"

"Already set," Chip told him. "I've been getting there ever since you stopped rolling dirt down."

"That's bully. Now I'm goin' to try and lass' yuh." He withdrew his head, picked up his rope and carefully shook out the loop, then let it down through the hole. In the dark like that it was partly guesswork, but Weary had skill in those supple young wrists of his. He swung the noose gently with a slow rotary motion to hold the loop open, and swift as a striking rattler he dropped it.

"Made it first throw. Pull!" Young Bennett's voice was not loud but it cracked a little under the strain of his emotion.

Weary Willie braced his heels against the top log of the cellar wall, leaned backward and pulled, hand over hand. It was harder than he had thought it would be. At first the drag was steady, then the rope jerked from side to side, giving him a horrible sensation of a man down there fighting for his breath. Panic-stricken, he slackened the pull a little.

"Y'all right?" he bent to ask anxiously.

47

"Fine. I was just getting my feet under me. Think you can make it?"

"Sure. Wait a minute. Can yuh stand there a second?"

"You bet."

Weary dropped the rope on the ground, ran the few steps to his horse, led the animal closer, picked up the loose coil and took a turn around the saddle horn. Then he spoke a word under his breath. As the trained rope horse walked slowly away against the pull of Chip's weight on the rope, Weary knelt on one knee alongside the hole, keeping his own half of the rope tight. Now the horse was doing the work, not he.

Three steps, and Chip's head came into sight. One more careful step and his shoulders rubbed the sides of the aperture. Weary caught him by one arm, and with one eye on the horse he eased Chip through, saw him stretched full length on the grass and said "Whoa!" in a tone that would not carry a dozen feet.

Without a word he flung off the loop that had caught under the bound arms, pulled his hunting knife from his belt and slashed the cruelly tight ropes with savage strokes. Then without a further word, he dragged Chip to the horse, heaved him across the saddle like a bag of meal and held him there with his shoulder while he recoiled his rope. It took perhaps ten seconds. Then he picked up the reins, lifted himself up behind the cantle, and rode away through the edge of the grove, heading down the flat toward the Whoop-up Trail. "I s'pose they got your gun," he observed glumly, when they were safely out of hearing from the house.

"I suppose so. One of them knocked me out. Let me

down, will you? Hell, I'm no cripple! I've got to go get my horses."

"Say, keep your shirt on, can't yuh?" Weary Willie admonished. "I'm heading for a clump of brush that's a jim-dandy hideout for yuh while I go round up your horses. Couldn't take a chance on your legs being numb—old Burch was liable to show up any minute. D' you hear that door slam just as I was draggin' you out? I did."

Chip did not reply to that, and almost immediately Weary turned aside and rode around a small thicket that, growing up around a fallen tree that had since rotted away, had a tiny clearing in its center. Into this he rode and slid to the ground. Young Bennett did the same, staggering as he attempted to stand alone.

"What'd I tell yuh?" snorted Weary. "Rub some feelin' into your arms an' legs while I sneak back after your horses. You can keep mine here. Any one come along, just lay low. They ain't liable to find yuh. I gotta have my gun."

He was leaving when Chip stopped him. "Say, you don't know my horses. There's my saddle horse and pack horse and a mare—"

"Yeah, I know," Weary cut him short. "Julie Lang told me."

"Oh." Chip let him go then, and Weary Willie faded into the blackness of the brushy flat.

Julie had sent him. Julie Lang. The music of her name thrilled Chip even in that hazardous moment. He walked carefully a few steps forward, a few steps back, worked his fingers and rubbed his arms. And he listened. But all the while he was thinking how a stranger had risked his life to rescue a man he didn't know from Adam's off ox, and had done it cheerfully because Julie Lang had asked him to. He must think a lot of Julie Lang, to do a thing like that. He must be Julie Lang's sweetheart. At that point young Chip Bennett said "Hell!" in a whisper, and closed a door of his mind upon Julie Lang.

He was standing by the horse, wondering what had gone wrong, looking and listening back the way they had come, when the horse turned his head and stared back the other way. Against the starlight Chip could see his ears tilted forward. Then he caught the swish of branches, the soft beat of many hoofs in the springy soil. And he was there with nothing but his two hands to fight with. He waited, one hand stroking the horse's nose to keep him quiet, feeling a little sick with the thought of his helplessness. True, he could mount and ride—a blind flight that could have but one finish. But he did nothing like that. He wouldn't run. He'd fight if he had to, but he wouldn't run.

The sounds came closer, seemed to be heading directly for where he stood. Then they stopped, all except a careless snapping of branches that seemed aimless and unnecessary. Then a muttered expostulation. "Hey, you darned little runt, get back where you belong!" And quiet footsteps advancing. "Y' all right, Chip?" the voice asked cautiously.

"So far I am. Did you get the horses, the mare and two colts?"

"You bet your sweet life I got 'em. Not a soul to stop

50

me; guess they must be settin' on your case. Had the bunch back up there in the brush in what the boys call Deadman's Corral—where they turn all the horses that's due to be orphans." Weary was leading the way to the horses, and while his voice was low and guarded, he appeared to be quite elated over his exploit. "Here y' are, feller. Don't think they touched a thing yet—never unsaddled or nothing. Burch is always real polite about a man's property. They always wait till after the hangin' before they settle the estate."

Chip grunted and swung up into the saddle. "They've got my gun, though, damn them."

"Yeah. Well, I couldn't go right in and take it off 'em," he apologized quaintly. "I didn't know just how they might take it. Might get sore or something."

For the first time young Bennett laughed boyishly. "You'll do," he said warmly. "Well, any advice to hand out before I go? If I knew where my brother is liable to be—"

"No telling," Weary said in a tone suddenly gruff. "I tell yuh what you do. There's a herd due here at the crossing any time now. An outfit up north here went to Billings to meet a shipment of mixed stock. You hit the high spots till you meet 'em—"

"That shouldn't be far," Chip interrupted. "There's been a herd trailing me for the last two days. They can't be out more than ten miles or so; maybe not that far."

"That's them, most likely. The Flying U. You go hunt 'em up and tell 'em Will Davidson sent yuh. Weary Willie. They'll know who yuh mean. Better tell 'em who you are and all about how the play come up. Jim

51

Whitmore'll back you up against Dave Burch and the whole shooting match here. He—"

"Jim Whitmore? Is he from Colorado?"

"Ain't sure—believe he is, though. You know him? Say, you're playing big luck if you know Jim Whitmore." They had reached the road, gray and empty in the starlight. Weary turned his head and listened. "Gosh, the luck sure is comin' our way. Maybe Milt talked 'em out of it. Couldn't take a chance on that, though. But they sure ain't raisin' any ruction over you bein' gone . . ." He hesitated, as if loath to go. "Well, so long. . . ."

Chip flung out a detaining hand. "Hold on a minute! I haven't tried to thank you—"

"It'll keep." Weary's teeth shone white in the starlight. He edged his horse into the trail. "I gotta drift. I aim to put in a long evening playin' checkers with Turk Bowles, down at the ferry. Any of them Vigilantes ketch me on the prowl, they might not trust me no more. You're all right now. Just keep foggin' right along till you hit the Flying U herd. You knowing Jim Whitmore—"

"The Jim Whitmore I mean sold out, down in Colorado. Said he was going to quit the cattle business. So—"

"So that's him, all right. J.G.'s always goin' to sell out, to hear him tell it. Well, so long." Before young Bennett could stop him, he was gone down the trail at a trot, leaning forward with his weight on the stirrups to ease the jolt. It had suddenly occurred to Weary Willie that the sooner he established an alibi for himself the better, because Dave Burch and Shaner certainly resented any opposition or interference with their authority as captain and lieutenant of the Vigilantes. If Milt failed to talk them over, they'd be right on the warpath.

Chip looked after him, watching until the slim boyish figure disappeared around a brushy bend in the trail. When he could no longer hear the soft *pluck-pluck-pluck* of the trotting hoofs, he reined Mike into the road, gave a yank on Jeff's lead rope and rode off toward the hills.

He had no more than got under way when a sound in the grove back of the Lang House prickled his scalp with a presentiment of evil. The eerie hoot of a horned owl three times repeated. But to Chip's tight-drawn nerves it had a human note; a signal of some kind, he would have sworn. The Vigilante warning that he had been missed, he guessed it.

His teeth came together as his mouth tightened. He tilted his spurs against Mike's flanks and was off in full flight, pulling Jeff and the mare and colts into a gallop as he rode.

6. Jim Whitmore Hires a Hand

AS THE FIRST GRAY LIGHT CREPT OVER THE PRAIRIE, A little brown bird cheeped and flew out of a bush as the horse herd came galloping up out of a hollow, the pleasant clamor of little bells riding the thunder of shod hoofs pounding the springy sod. Manes tossing in the dawn wind, they went scurrying past, harried by the hie-hie and the perfunctory epithets of the night hawk.

Half a mile back toward the silvering east a great dark blot moved vaguely as the herd awoke, the more enterprising animals already walking out from the mass, nosing the trampled sod as they went. Cows were lumbering awkwardly to their feet that hungry calves might bunt and suckle. Two riders edged out away from the herd to let the cattle spread out and graze. They rode under a changing canopy of purple and rose and orange that drew even their accustomed eyes to gaze upon its glory.

The dawn light touched the camp, giving the weathered tents a rosy hue. As the jingling remuda trotted up and ducked into the rope corral, a stocky man of middle age came stooping out between the flaps of the bed tent. Behind him came young Bennett, looking as if he still lay under the spell of that horror which he had so narrowly escaped.

He moved to the corral, picked up the trailing rope and tied it to its iron stake, shutting the horses inside the slight barrier. The night hawk thanked him with a grin and a casual gesture which did not entirely conceal his curiosity. His glance turned inquiringly toward the strange horses picketed out beyond the mess wagon where they would be hidden from sight of any one riding out from the trail, but he did not say anything. Nor did Chip.

The stocky man came over and stood beside him. "Purty fair bunch of horses," he observed with a studied carelessness that plainly wanted to put the boy at his ease. "I'll pick yuh out a string of good cowhorses purty soon. That big roan right next to the gray, there, is wise as they make 'em. I guess you better ride him this morning."

"If you think it's liable to make any trouble for you or your outfit, Mr. Whitmore—"

"No trouble at all. Better git washed up. Breakfast'll be ready in two shakes."

Other cowboys came straggling from the bed tent, sidelong glances sizing up the stranger who had routed the boss out of his blankets last night for a long and low-voiced "conflab" well out away from the tent. Jim Whitmore toweled his face vigorously, looked from one to the other while he dried his hands.

"Boys, this is Chip Bennett, just up from Colorado," he announced, nodding toward Chip, who was carefully washing his swollen jaw. "Used to know him when he was a little shaver." And he added in a tone that made his men look at him, "Lookin' for his brother—Wane Bennett." He shot a keen glance around the group. "Meantime, he rides with the outfit." And to break the tension, he added quizzically, "I guess you can ride, can't yuh? I forgot to ask."

"Well, I didn't walk all the way from Denver," Chip retorted, looking up with face and hair dripping. Then he blushed at his own temerity. "Yes, sir, I've had a little experience on round-ups."

"You'll get more, most likely," his new boss made dry comment, and moved to obey the cook's call to breakfast.

Through the meal the cowboys eyed Chip covertly, taking due notice of the empty holster on his belt, the bruised and swollen jaw, the bleak look in his eyes. If they said little, he had even less to say. And yet their silence was friendly enough and he lost a little of the hard wariness from his eyes and mouth before the meal was over. A good meal, better than his own makeshift cooking, and he ate hungrily and listened to the desultory sentences that concerned their work and their affairs.

After that, an orderly confusion pervaded the camp. Men caught and saddled their horses and rode out to the herd to relieve the guard, who galloped in to their breakfast. Others pulled down the tents, rolled them expertly and loaded the two wagons. Chip caught the big roan and saddled him, then stood waiting for orders.

"Throw them horses of yours into the remuda," Jim Whitmore told him crisply. "They'll cross ahead of the cattle. Nobody'll git a second squint at 'em."

Chip picked up the reins, looked over to where little Silver was industriously breakfasting, hind legs spraddled, bushy red tail waggling. His eyes grew worried. "That colt's awful little to swim such a wide river," he demurred. "I was going to take the mare and colts over on the ferry, if I had to cross."

Jim Whitmore's chuckle was full of assurance. "Sure, if yuh want to advertise 'em, go ahead. But that colt'd fool yuh, son, if he got in swimmin' water. Swim like a duck. Anyway, it ain't likely he'll have to swim a stroke. Good, rock-bottom ford. Hadn't oughta be belly deep to a duck today."

"Oh." Chip heaved a deep sigh of relief. "That's all right, then. But I sure think a lot of that little devil. He's mine. The other two belong to Wane, as I told you."

If Whitmore heard that last sentence, he gave no sign as he turned away toward the horse wrangler who was mounting to take the remuda on out of camp. "Bennett's horses go into the bunch, Happy. Kinda keep an eye on them two colts; they got good blood in 'em. Slim, you and Penny go along and help with the horses. Hold 'em back on the edge of the flat where that clearing is, till the cattle get there. We'll push down to the river just ahead of the herd and shove 'em across." He hesitated, glanced at Chip who was coiling his picket ropes, swung to the grouped cowboys again.

"They glommed that kid last night when he rode in, askin' for his brother Wane," he stated grimly. "That young Davidson, over at the Lazy Ladder, pulled him outa their damn cellar b'fore they got around to hang him. They claimed he'd stole that mare and colts up on the Musselshell and altered the brand from LP. That's a damn lie."

"There's an LP over on the Musselshell," the man called Penny—his name was August Penn—remarked in a tone meant to be neutral.

"I don't give a damn if there's forty LP irons in the country; I knew that mare when she was a filly. She's an EB and she always has been, and I'll go to the ground with anybody that says she ain't."

"The kid heard about his brother?" Cal Emmett wanted to know.

"No, and he ain't goin' to—not in this camp. Git started, boys. Keep them horses back away from Lang's till I say the word, and then send 'em across hell a-whoopin'. The kid'll ride with me."

He strode over to where the night hawk and the cook were preparing to start off with their four-horse teams and the two wagons. "Pull out in the clearing at the edge of the flat and wait till the herd gits by," he ordered. "You bring up the drag t'day. I'm liable to need you fellers." They looked at him, but he would not vouchsafe any explanations.

The herd was moving up, walking briskly without stopping to graze. They had not watered since noon the day before and they were thirsty enough to string out and walk steadily as yoked oxen to the river. Slim and Penny lifted themselves into their saddles, reined sharply aside to head off a few investigative horses wandering out away from the bunch. They swung rope ends, yelled "Git back there!" adding casual expletives as a matter of habit. The remuda swirled and started off with a thudding of quick hoof beats. A lean sorrel lifted his heels to a chunky black he had a grudge against, and the black ducked up and nipped him on the neck in revenge. Penny yelled again the thing he would do if they didn't cut out that monkey business.

Chip's gaze followed his own horses. They were sticking together at the tail of the bunch, Jeff and Mike blending nicely in with the other bays and browns. Silvia and her colts were pretty darn conspicuous with their creamy manes and tails. A mare and colt looked out of place in a bunch of round-up horses, anyway. The way they were striking out for the river, it looked to Chip as though little Silver was going to be all tuckered out before they got there, and he wouldn't get his dinner when he wanted it. You couldn't expect those

58

cowboys to hold up the whole bunch just to let Silver suck.

Rummy was all right, only he stood out like a sore thumb in that bunch of cayuses. Rummy was prancing along, looking as important as sin. Thought he was a real horse, running with the Flying U remuda like that. If they tried any funny business with that young feller, Mr. Rummy would plant his heels in their ribs and be gone somewhere else before they knew what had happened. Streak of greased lightning, that silver-maned little devil.

The herd trooped down a slope and disappeared in a winding wash. The cattle came up, plodding forward under a gray banner of dust. A big man called Shorty rode point, walking his horse alongside a huge white ox with wide horns gracefully curved backward. Jim Whitmore sat his horse, eyeing the long procession as it passed. With eyes half shut and face that told nothing, he looked at Chip and with the flip of a hand gestured him to his station.

Chip swung in alongside the herd. The wind had risen with the sun and was blowing down and across the herd as they walked into its invisible, swift-flowing stream. He rode in dust so thick his mouth was gritty with it, his long dark lashes clogged with dirt. In half an hour even Shaner would have hesitated to point to that slim rider on the tall roan and say there went the youth he had called a horse thief only yesterday. But if that had been Jim Whitmore's purpose, no man would ever know.

They struck the Whoop-up Trail where it snaked down through the broken land to the willow flat below.

They passed the round-up wagons in the open glade, where Chip had made his last camp the day before, thinking of Julie Lang while he ate fried grouse and drank black coffee from a battered tin cup. Ahead, the horse bells jangled cheerfully down the trail. He heard Silvia's bell-like whinny, calling Rummy back from reckless ventures of his own.

Chip's throat tightened. A matter of minutes now and they would be at the river. They would rush that colt of his in with the rest, and he was too little and too tired to hold his own amongst those range-bred cayuses. Even Rummy was scarcely equal to the ordeal, or gentle Silvia who had never taken the hard knocks of range life.

How Chip suffered during that next hour of dust and clamor, the bawling of anxious cows worried about their calves, the yells and the shrill vituperations of the cowboys, no one was permitted to suspect. He dashed here and there on the big roan, hazing cattle out of the brush and yelling with the rest. His shrill *"Hie! Hie! Hi-eah! Git along there, you this-and-thats!"* carried as far as any voice among the riders—though it must be admitted his language came much nearer being print-able than did any of the others. Still, he cussed the cattle like a real hand, and he won a secret grin from Jim Whitmore, who was keeping an eye on him.

Then they were at the river, splashing into the ford. Deeper, deeper, the big roan snatching a drink as he waded in. Up to the stirrups, so he had to pull out his feet and tuck them up along the saddle skirts. Current flowing with a swift steady push, making tiny wavelets on the upstream side of his horse. The calves were swimming, awash to their stubby noses and wide-straining eyeballs. Each one swimming close alongside its mother, right against her shoulder, she taking that resistless push of the current, the water up to her chin, with her head stretched out. (Little Silver—even Rummy would have to swim, Chip thought, with sickening weight in his chest.)

How wide was the damn thing, anyway? Belly deep to a duck! Hell! Up ahead there, dozens of cattle had lost their footing off the ford and were swimming for their lives, nose and eyes and horns showing above the relentless sweep of the grayish water; snorting and snuffling as they swam, the pudgy faces of scared calves valiantly kept pace with their mothers. The yelling cowboys let them go in seeming unconcern, trusting to shrewd animal instinct to bring them all safe ashore.

How wide was it, anyway? Over the backs of the wading cattle Chip stared strainingly ahead. They didn't seem to be a damn bit closer to shore. Maybe Silvia had gone off the ford like those cows. It certainly was an awful long ways to expect a two-months-old colt to swim, especially after he'd had to keep up with a round-up remuda for a couple of hours beforehand. If he had known what he knew now, he'd have chanced another run-in with those damned fellows; he'd have taken Silvia and the colts across on the ferry.

Then suddenly the shore looked very near. The water dropped from the roan's shoulders to the stirrups, to the horse's knees. The swimming cattle found hard river bottom under their feet and forged up and out on the trodden gravel bank. The dripping calves gave each leg a comical shake, like a cat coming out of snow, switched their tails and trotted after their mothers.

Chip's feet dropped, toes feeling for the stirrups and thrusting in. The big roan grunted as he heaved himself up the sloping bank. Ahead, the cattle were spreading a little; cowboys galloped and yelled, *"Hie! Hie! Hieah!"* adding picturesque upbraidings as they rode with high flapping elbows, spurred horses leaping ahead to turn some animal suddenly bolting for freedom. Behind him the remainder of the herd came wading, swimming, straining to reach the shore. In midstream the stoutrailed ferry came sidling across, nose snubbed to the great cable and the current for once put to work helping instead of hindering the crossing. Tied short, so they could not lunge, the four-horse teams leaned away from the edge and with wild, staring eyeballs watched the sliding river.

Riding well behind Chip for reasons of his own, Jim Whitmore came up out of the water and overtook the boy, who was craning and looking this way and that, trying to discover the remuda. "Well, yuh made it all right, didn't yuh? Wasn't a soul come near us. If Burch is lookin' for yuh, he sure never had any idea you'd ever show up again at the river."

"No, I guess not," said Chip, to whom the whole affair of last night had become rather far away and unreal, in the face of the peril his beloved colts had just suffered. "I'd like to ride out to the remuda and see if everything's all right, Mr. Whitmore. I'll be right back."

Jim Whitmore stared, gave an unintelligible grunt and a gesture of permission, and wheeled back to see that the wagons came ashore all right. Patsy's leaders were liable to cut up, getting off that ferry. Anyway, he had to pay Turk Bowles for crossing 'em. That young devil of a Bennett boy either had nerve, or he was light in the upper story. Worried more over them dawgoned colts than he did over his own neck.

The horse herd, wet and showing rough and dirty hides where most of them had rolled since coming out of the water, were feeding quietly in a grassy coulee nearly a mile from the river. Close grouped, the three men in charge were talking with a fourth who had just ridden up. They eyed Chip with interest as he rode over and dismounted beside his own horses, grazing off by themselves with that clannishness so thoroughly characteristic of horses which have trailed or worked together for a time.

They looked up, nickered their welcome and crowded round him, begging for sugar. Little Silver was wet to his ears, but he seemed none the worse for his adventure and was avidly at work getting his dinner and bunting reproof when Silvia moved up a step to meet her master. Chip's eyes brightened at the sight of him, and his tight mouth relaxed and recovered its boyish curve. He was handing out lumps of cut-loaf sugar and fondly berating Rummy when the strange rider left the Flying U boys and came trotting over.

"Hello! Made the riffle all right, I see." His grin was wide and friendly. "I'm the guy that hauled yuh outs the cellar last night," he added, when Chip's eyes failed to light with recognition.

"Oh. Weary Willie, hunh?" They studied each other. "I owe you a big debt of gratitude, all right. I—"

"Maybe so, maybe not. You ain't outa the woods yet, if I'm any judge uh snakes. My boss claims I done yuh more damage by draggin' you outa there than if I'd left yuh in. I kinda put my foot in it, I guess. I shouldn't of horned in like that."

"No? He wanted me hung, did he?"

"No, he says not. He'd went and talked 'em into letting you go. He was going to take yuh to his place— stand good for yuh till they could find out for sure about that mare and colts. If they proved you'd stole 'em, he'd have to turn yuh over to 'em, uh course. That was the bargain. And then," Weary grinned, "the scheme fell through, on account of me gettin' nosey and rescuing you. Don't it beat hell, Chip?"

Chip's straight dark eyebrows came together in a frown. "Jim Whitmore can prove that mare's an EB, all right. He knows her. What I don't savvy is that boss of yours. Why should he get tender-hearted over a fellow he never' saw in his life?"

Weary Willie chuckled. "He didn't. You know Julie Lang? Well, Milt's been sweet on her for a coon's age. They was engaged, I heard, and busted it up. She had Milt go make a talk for you."

"Oh." A glow came into Chip's face. "It was her work, then."

"Yeah. She told me about you and sent me off to tell Milt she wanted to see him right away. So I told him, all right, and then I took a notion it'd be just as well not to bank too heavy on what Milt could do. So I kinda spoiled Milt's play, see? And he's mad as a hornet," Weary sighed. "I've got to hunt me a new job. Think I'll strike J.G. for a place on his pay roll."

"Jim Whitmore? I wish you would."

Weary's eyes brightened. "Sure will. There's liable to be a scrap over you yet, and if there is, I want to be in on it."

By tacit agreement they had left the horses and were riding together back toward the river. Chip was busy thinking, chewing a corner of his lip and staring straight ahead of him. From time to time Weary glanced at him inquiringly, but he did not speak until they passed the grazing herd and were nearing the wagons where smoke was already rising from the dinner fire. "We'll likely find J.G. in camp," he observed then, and twitched the reins, sending his horse that way.

"Tell him I'll be back pretty soon," Chip called after him. "Tell him I've gone back across the river. I've got business with those two exponents of the law, over there." He touched spurs to the roan and was off down the trail to the ford, while Weary stared blankly after him.

7. Chip Takes a Chance

GRAY CURRENT SWEEPING LEVEL WITH HIS CHEST, THE big roan waded valiantly across. Chip rode relaxed. No need to worry now about the colts or Silvia. With his mind's clear eye he saw them, glossy coats shining against the green sloping up to rocks and brush; apart from the herd, yet protected by it and the watchful eyes of the cowboys. Those two extra men were there on their account, he knew. And with this big river flowing between them and Dave Burch, and the Flying U camp just back from the shore—they were dead safe.

As for himself, he scarcely thought of any danger in this errand. He was riding a Flying U horse, and the Flying U outfit was just over there, with Jim Whitmore ready to vouch for him if he needed it. They'd think twice today before they tried to play any Vigilante tricks on him.

A freight outfit stood before Lang's place. Boxes and barrels and kegs were being unloaded for store and saloon. A wagon was pulling up in front of the blacksmith shop. Two horsemen were just leaving, galloping down the flat toward the Whoop-up Trail, all scarred now with the passing of the herd. Back at the edge of the grove, hidden from the settlement by the Lang house and outbuildings, a woman in a blue dress was bending over some work in a fenced garden patch. As Chip rode up out of the river, he heard the shrill staccato barking of a small dog he knew must be Tiny.

With one glance he took a complete survey of the place—and suddenly recognized that slight figure in blue. With a twist of the rein he turned back and swung down from the saddle at the water's edge. Partly concealed by his horse, he squatted there and scooped water in his two hands, washing his face and neck and ears with meticulous care, drying them with his handkerchief. He pulled off his black neckerchief, shook it vigorously, refolded it and knotted it neatly in a four-in-hand style. He fished a pocket comb from an inner coat pocket and dipped it three times in the river between combings, trying to coax the wave out of his hair. He picked up his gray range hat, beat the dust from it against his chaps, dented it just so and set it carefully on his damp hair, with just the hint of a rakish tilt. Then, and then only, he picked up the reins and remounted. He was glad that the stink of those old potatoes last night had impelled him to pull a clean shirt out of his warbag and put it on.

With due thought for the fat and fault-finding aunt, he rode along the trail until he was opposite the garden patch, and then turned sharply aside and headed straight for it, hoping he was well out of range from the windows.

Julie Lang was weeding onions, pulling the largest for the table as she went stooping down the row. She wore a blue chambray sunbonnet that matched her dress, and the starched front, like blinds on a horse, restricted her vision to what was directly in front of her. Until she looked up to scold the hysterically yapping Tiny, she did not see young Bennett at all. "Oh!" she gasped, standing up straight and staring at him. "You scared me. What—where in the world did you come from?"

"Just across the river." Chip swung a long and limber leg over the cantle and came down in a tangle of young sunflowers and soap weed. "I saw you up here, so I just stopped to say—"

"But you mustn't!" She darted a frightened glance across to the blacksmith shop. "Oh, why didn't you stay away when you got the chance?" Her tone was almost tragic in its dismay.

Chip folded his arms upon the fence's top rail, the bridle reins dangling loosely from his fingers. The sight of her went to his head a little. Shy though he was, her stammering confusion made him feel suddenly bold and masterful. "That sounds as if you were kind of sorry you saved my life," he said, with a half-amused twist of his lips.

Julie ignored the challenge. "I suppose it was Will Davidson got you out. They were all ready to let you go, and then he had to spoil it all by helping you escape!"

"He never spoiled anything for me, anyway." Chip's slow smile was born with a twinkle in his eyes. "I wasn't in any position to take a chance on their having a change of heart."

Julie shook her head with a baffled impatience. "I know—nobody could blame you. I can't, anyway. But it made it look as if you were guilty and couldn't stand investigating. Don't you know, Chip, you're taking an awful chance, right this minute? If Dave Burch over there should look this way—"

"Let him. He'd see a man on a Flying U horse, stopping to talk to you a minute. No crime in that, is there? Flying U cowboys have got a right to talk to you, haven't they?"

"Flying U?" She stared at him in bewilderment. "I thought you were alone."

"I was—yesterday. But I know Jim Whitmore. If they jump me again about those horses, I've got a witness to

68

prove where they came from. They can't do a thing but back down."

"Oh. Can't they?" Julie gave him an odd, searching look.

"Nothing but look foolish and maybe apologize." Chip was so engrossed with the girl's beauty that her look and tone escaped him.

She picked up the pestiferous little dog and held him in her arms as she walked up to the fence and stood leaning against it. The roan thrust out his nose to snuff at the dog, which set up so terrific a clamor that Julie set him down and spanked him, sending him off with his absurd little tail between his pipestem legs.

"There's something I wanted to ask you about, Julie." Chip was shy with girls, but shyness sometimes surprises itself by seeming overbold. As she stood there beside him, her shoulder was quite close. He lifted a curl that rested near his hand. Like golden silk it felt.

"What is it? If it's about Shaner or Dave Burch, I can't—"

"It's not. It's about my brother Wane. You know him, you told me. Well enough so he talked to you about me, and that means you were pretty good friends. He's a lot like me, I guess; it's kinda hard for us to talk much about ourselves except—unless we like a person quite a lot. He ain't here, he's gone somewhere, but nobody I've asked seems to know anything much about him; where he went or anything. I thought maybe—didn't he tell you, Julie?"

The blue sunbonnet did not turn Chip's way, but her shoulder moved a little, making the curl in his fingers seem alive and friendly. He wanted to lift it against his mouth, but he was not quite bold enough for that.

"No-o, he didn't tell me, Chip."

"It's darn funny. He—I'll bet he liked you a lot, Julie. He couldn't help it, you're so—just the kind of girl he'd be mashed on. Wasn't he?"

"You don't expect me to answer a question like that, do you?" Julie's voice sounded as if it came through closed teeth.

"Well, no, I guess not. If you did, and it was yes, I'd sure be jealous of Wane."

"You needn't be, silly."

"Or—of anybody else?"

"Not if you had any common sense."

Chip sighed and picked up another curl, twisting the two together. "I guess I haven't got any sense at all—where you're concerned."

Silence, vibrating with emotions utterly beyond speech.

"I guess you think I'm seventeen kinds of a fool."

And after a breathless pause—"You know I don't."

"Honest?" Chip picked up a third curl, smoothed it with fingers that had kisses in their tips. "This is only the third time—but you saved my life. Even if you hadn't, I'd have felt the same, anyway—"

"I didn't save it. I'm worried to death this minute, for fear I've made you trouble. I never dreamed Will Davidson would—"

"You haven't made me any trouble at all." Chip was braiding the three shining curls together, smoothing each tress down until it shone like polished gold.

"Yes, I have. Because now—" Julie did not go on.

"You haven't, because now I won't be obligated to a fellow that stood up for me because he was stuck on you. I guess you don't realize how I'd have felt about that." He finished the braiding and began carefully undoing his work again. "You meant it all right, I know that. You just thought about helping me. But—I'd sure hate to owe my life to a man just because he—loved you." The word made his cheeks hot, but with her face hidden inside that starched bonnet, he was much less shy than if she were looking at him.

"You don't know—that he does."

"I've got a darned good guess. If he ain't blind, he'd sure have to."

"He's mad enough now," Julie said cryptically.

"Mad at me, or at you—or both of us?" No girl in the world had ever won that hushed intimate tone from Chip Bennett.

"At me, because I won't stick to a bargain we made. But he didn't carry out his side of it, so that lets me out. Isn't that right?"

"It sure is, if he didn't live up to it either. What—"

"Oh, it wasn't anything much," said Julie hastily, forestalling the question she wouldn't answer. Perhaps she felt the little tug at her hair; she moved an inch closer and then stood very still. "Milt's a nice fellow and everybody likes him. But I just can't stand any one that tries to be domineering and—and doesn't play fair. He just talked awful because I said the bargain was off. And he was the first one to break it, too."

"Hunh! " snorted Chip. "If that's the kind of a hairpin

he is, I'm certainly glad I'm not under any obligations to him."

"So am I," murmured Julie. "Only, I wouldn't want you to get into trouble over me. He might try to start a fuss with you; he'd do it just to spite me."

"Let him try it!" Chip said darkly. "If he says any more about it, you let me know. Will you— Goldilocks?"

"Oh!" She turned and pushed back her bonnet, looking up big-eyed into his face. "How did—what made you call me that, Chip? That's what—Wane— always called me."

A pang that was half ecstasy shot along Chip's veins. The hazel tints in his eyes seemed to catch the glow of some hidden fire as he stared deep into the cloudy blue of her eyes. When he spoke, his voice had a huskily vibrant timbre utterly strange to it.

"Maybe he felt the same as I do—only he couldn't; nobody could." And he added, with the shy boyish candor that only her near presence could wring from him, "I never saw anybody like you before. Like a poem had come to life—Tennyson's Maud or—or the Princess. Or a picture. I—I draw pictures, myself. I'll try and make one of you, only I know I never could make it beautiful as you are. Like a dawn sky. This morning, for instance. Did you see it? The beauty of it kind of chokes a fellow. And that's the way I felt the first time I ever saw you—back there when you went past in the rig. Like music you dream about—or more like this morning. Or a sunset. Anything that's so wonderful it makes your throat ache—"

Julie looked utterly enthralled by his halting rhapsody. She must have listened to many declarations of love, but never one just like this. A boy's declaration, worshipful, terribly sincere.

He was staring hard into her face, lost to all else. "I don't know what magic you've got. You pulled me all the way from Denver. I thought it was because I wanted to find Wane and tell him—about mother dying, and to be with him. It was that—partly. But most of all it was because you were up here, pulling me to you. Little Goldilocks!"

For a moment Julie's eyes glowed up at him like two purple pansies transfigured by angels. Her red mouth quivered as if it hungered for his kisses. Then she looked away, pulling her sunbonnet over her face as if she were deliberately quenching the beauty that whipped his emotions to such ardor. "We're both of us crazy, standing here talking like this. We've got everybody gawping over here at us. You'd better go back to the Flying U and stay there till things kind of die down."

Had she dashed a dipper of cold water in his face, the shock would have been less. Chip took his arms off the fence and stepped back so abruptly he startled the roan. With a jerk of the reins he brought him back, thrust boot toe to stirrup and swung up. From the saddle he looked down at Julie Lang with much the same aloofness he had shown the freighter who laughed at him. "I've got nothing to hide from or to be ashamed of," he said coldly. "Not even talking like a fool just now. I expect you think I'm crazy—"

"Oh, for heaven's sake! Can't you see I'm simply scared to death for you—your safety? And there comes Milt, up from the ferry. Do you *want* to make trouble for me—dear?"

That last word swept away his defenses. "I'll come again when there isn't so much gawp seed for sale. Don't be afraid, little Goldilocks. Anybody harms you, he'll have to answer to me!"

The swift pluckety-pluckety of Milt Cummings' horse was in his ears as he wheeled and rode across the street, but he did not deign a glance that way. Nor did he know that he had left damning evidence of his wooing for Milt to see and take note of,—three shining yellow curls neatly braided together in a tight pigtail there on Julie's shoulder.

8. Like a Wolf and a Grizzly

THE LITTLE KNOT OF MEN BEFORE THE BLACKSMITH shop eyed him in silence. Dave Burch's cold stare was like the hunting gaze of a hawk as Chip pulled up the roan ten feet from the doorway. Ginger-whiskered Shaner came at a trot from the stable near by. Burch's right hand hovered close to his holster.

Chip's eyes were boring into the bearded face. "Captain Burch, I came after that gun you took away from me last night."

"Did, ay? You've got your gall, showin' up here again, young feller."

"Yes?" A strong vein of sarcasm in Chip's nature lent a maddening flavor of contempt to the word.

"You can cut out the impudence," Burch said harshly, taking a forward step. "You was placed under arrest last night on strong suspicion of bein' a horse thief, and was bein' held pendin' an investigation and trial. You proved your guilt by makin' your escape." Before the small audience he adopted the cold, measured tones of a judge. He seemed very sure of his ground, and it was plain that the three or four strangers were impressed.

"Poppycock!" snapped Chip. "Anybody would get out of that damned cellar of rotten potatoes if he could. I proved my innocence by coming back after my gun, didn't I?" From the tail of his eye he saw the strangers look at one another in approval. He had scored a point there, and he decided to clinch it while he could. "If I'd been guilty, you couldn't have seen my trail for dust, and you know it."

"What you done with that mare and two colts you stole?" Shaner broke in. "Got 'em hid out in the brush, I s'pose!"

"That mare and colts you *claim* I stole are in the Flying U remuda, where they're going to stay. Jim Whitmore's looking after 'em for me, if it's anything to you. You can ask him whether I stole 'em or not. He knew that mare down in Colorado."

"That's what *you* claim. He ain't here to back yuh up on that statement, I notice."

"I'm riding a Flying U horse, you notice." Chip reached back and slapped the roan's sleek rump significantly. "This brand talks for me all I need."

Burch shook his head judiciously. "The charge against you ain't wiped off the slate yet, young feller;

75

not by a long row of stumps. Shaner here accused you of havin' a stolen mare and two colts, and it ain't been proved yet you're innocent of the charge. I'll have to hold you till we git this thing settled to the satisfaction of a jury."

"Yeah, and this time I won't talk myself black in the face getting you to turn him loose on no probation," a voice behind Chip spoke up. "You may not be dry behind the ears yet, but you sure don't act like no novice to me, when it comes to devilment. Chances are you throwed a long loop for that horse you're ridin' right now."

Chip turned his head and looked into the handsome face of Milt Cummings. "Another county heard from," he drawled insolently. "You must be aiming for a place on the jury!"

"Yeah. Make it a coroner's jury, and I'd be tickled t' death to oblige," Milt taunted. Though he made no sign of it, Chip knew that he also was playing for the approval of the men standing by and taking it all in; just as Burch had been doing all along.

With his next sentence, Milt proved it. " 'Cause why? I'll tell yuh. I went and talked my fool head off last night, bailing you out. Got the captain here to put you in my care, me standin' good for yuh, till they had time to send to the Musselshell and get an LP man down here to look at that mare. And what does you do? Make a sneak while I was arguin' about your youth and inno-cence—and left me holdin' the bag!"

As their angry eyes met, both knew that this was not the reason why Milt Cummings hated him. Chip shrugged expressive shoulders and turned back to Dave Burch.

"Mr. Burch, you stand for honesty and justice—so I'd like my gun. You know well enough I'm no horse thief. I'm working for the Flying U. Jim Whitmore knows me. He knew my father and my brother—"

"And if that's the case, why ain't he here to say so himself?" sneered Shaner.

"Because I didn't tell him I was coming. It oughta be enough that I did come, and that I'm riding a Flying U horse."

"It shore ain't enough for me," declared Shaner; but Burch waved him down.

"Better get Whitmore over here an' see what he's got t' offer," one of the bystanders suggested, spitting tobacco juice in the general direction of Shaner.

The man at his elbow nodded. "The young feller talks purty straight, Cap'n, sounds like t' me."

Chip turned and looked down at them, a grateful glance. "It *is* straight. The trail herd just crossed the river awhile ago. While they camped for dinner, I thought I'd better get my gun back while we're this close. It belonged to my father and I want it back."

Burch plucked at his long, graying beard. "I've got nothin' so far but your own say-so. That ain't enough. You're purty bold-actin' fer a law-abidin' feller that ain't any older than you be, but it takes more'n talk to explain some things around here. I ain't satisfied—"

"Better hand the boy his gun, Burch." From just beyond the freight wagon that had hidden his approach, Jim Whitmore spoke with calm authority. He rode up alongside Chip, giving Milt Cummings a cursory glance and nod as he brushed past. Behind him rode his cowboys; seven of them, with their guns hanging snug at their sides and their right hands ungloved and resting negligently on their right thighs; with their hats tilted at a rakish angle and the light of pleased expectancy in their eyes.

J.G. leaned forward with his left forearm on his saddle horn, and while he spoke in a conversational tone there was a steely look in his eyes. "I knew this boy when he was just a little shaver. Knew his father—know all about him and his horses. There ain't a mean bone in his body. And that mare you're makin' such a fuss about I've known since she was a two-year-old. "If that gun he's askin' for is the one his dad used to pack, it's got silver trimmin' and an ivory butt with a steer's head carved on it. Kinda fancy to look at, but it sure is a gogetter in action. That it, Mr. Burch?"

"I—yes, I believe it is." Burch drew himself up with all the dignity of his position. "Since you are willing to vouch for the young man, and identify the mare, I'll dismiss the charge against him. My only desire," he added elegantly, "is to serve justice."

"Well, hell, go ahead and serve her!" snorted Whitmore. "Dig up that gun. We've got a trail herd on our hands."

While Burch was gone into the blacksmith shop, the Flying U boss looked at Shaner. "You the man that made the charge against this boy?" he inquired bluntly.

Shaner stood his ground. "I'm shore the man," he said, with a malevolent leer in his eyes. "One damn

78

horse thief he claims to be a brother of, was strung up, an' this one's goin' to end up the same way. Them Bennetts are bad med—"

"You damned, lying—!" So swiftly no man there saw just how he did it, Chip leaped from the roan and struck the word back in Shaner's tobacco-stained teeth. "If you—hung Wane—I'll—*kill*—every man—that had a hand in it!" For every pause a frenzied blow. And after that he fought in silence, his face no longer boyish but a grinning, blazing-eyed mask of ruthless vengeance.

Burch, Milt Cummings, started forward to pull him off. They made but the one move to show their intent. Then the Flying U boys rode in and herded every man back out of the way. They did not say anything, nor did they offer any other assistance save the silent menace of their seven guns. To a man they seemed to know that the boy's whole future, his very sanity perhaps, hung upon each blow he struck now for Wane.

Like a young wolf pitted against a grizzly, he fought. He was eighteen, six feet tall and slim, with wiry muscles hardened by school athletics and two months on the trail; eighteen, galvanized by the shock of the most horrible sentence he had ever heard from the mouth of a man.

And Shaner was short, stocky, powerful, with twenty years of rough fighting behind him. To him it was just a fight with a young whelp he could whip with one hand tied behind him. A young catamount on the warpath—but he knew all the tricks. The agonizing lift of the knee, the stiffened thumb to gouge out an eye, the throttling strangle hold. Mayhem was never barred, as far as Shaner was concerned, and if he could get the kid over to that wagon tongue he meant to break his damned back for him. That was Shaner in a fight.

And then Jim Whitmore leaned forward and leveled his sixshooter almost in the man's face as he pushed and struggled, Chip's head clamped under one arm. "Break away!" rasped J.G. "One dirty move and I'll blow your damned head off!"

Shaner rolled a glance up from under his pale eyebrows and released Chip so abruptly that the boy fell and lay dazed for ten seconds. Shaner's foot raised itself automatically and by force of habit, but he did not jump on Chip's unprotected middle and crush his ribs in, as he would have done as a matter of course. Instead, he set his foot down behind him, stepping back and away, until Chip staggered to his feet. Even then, with Jim Whitmore's gun bleakly regarding the back of his head, he waited until Chip had shaken the whirring wheels from his head and came at him again.

But the end was much the same. With his fists he punished Chip cruelly, grinning while he placed his blows. Yet Chip fought on, half blinded as his eyelids puffed. His swollen mouth grinned hate. There came an unexpected diversion that ended the fight. A blue whirlwind swept in between Weary Willie and Milt Cummings. Bareheaded, braided pigtails comically conspicuous among her yellow curls, Julie Lang tore at Shaner's sweaty, red flannel shirt. Her small weed-stained hands released his collar and beat upon his bullet head. "You brute! You beast! You've killed and crippled enough men, Tom Shaner! Shame on you, beating a boy just out of school! Pick some one your age and equal, if you must fight! "

Again Shaner rolled his eyes sidewise, looked into the round black eye of J.G. Whitmore's gun and stepped back, his hands at his sides. But he snarled an oath and a protest. "Git this Jezebel away from here and leave me be! How'n hell can a man fight in this kinda jackpot? Take 'er away!"

Through slits between his swollen lids, Chip Bennett peered at Julie. "Get outa the way and let me kill him!" he cried hoarsely. "You heard what he said, didn't you?" He referred, of course, to the horrible statement concerning Wane, and that remark Julie had not heard. She thought they were fighting over what had happened last night, and she would not yield an inch.

She still slapped and clawed at Shaner, though she spoke to Chip. "I won't go away! Haven't you got any sense? He's *killed* men with his hands—and his feet. Just look at you—beaten to a pulp!" She whirled suddenly upon the ringed cowboys with their guns, at Jim Whitmore covering Shaner. She stamped her foot. Her eyes were no longer purple pansies turned into stars. They were black and stormy. "And you!" she cried shrilly. "Cowards! Brutes, every one of you! Sitting there and grinning and taking in the show! And you, Milt Cummings, is this the way you save him and protect him? You make Shaner leave him alone, I tell you—or I'll never speak to you again as long as I live!"

"I don't want any man's protection!" Chip mumbled angrily. "Go away, Goldilocks, and let me finish him!" Perhaps it was fortunate his torn lip made for poor artic-

81

ulation. In that crowd, with Milt sitting his horse twelve feet or so away, calling the girl Goldilocks was a great mistake; or would have been, had any man there understood him.

Julie's back being turned for the moment, and all eyes fixed upon her in discomfiture as she lashed them with her tongue, Shaner returned single-mindedly to the issue. "Finish me, ay?" he snarled between closed teeth, and struck with all his strength behind the blow.

He lifted Chip, sent him down as he had done at the hitch rail yesterday. Too late Julie heard the thud of fist on jaw, and whirled. Then Barr Lang arrived and got a firm grip on her shoulder and pulled her out of the scene with a grim authority she could not but obey.

Chip lay where he had fallen. His face was a pitiful series of purpling contusions. His eyes were swollen nearly shut, his upper lip had been torn between fist and teeth. Blood was on his shirt that had been clean that morning. Blood was spattered on his fringed leather chaps. His spurred boots had not escaped. And he was completely unconscious.

Jim Whitmore looked at him, lifted his gun and looked for Shaner. But Shaner had vanished from sight. He turned his attention to Dave Burch. "Which way'd he go? He hit the kid when the kid wasn't looking. Where is he, Burch?"

Burch looked vaguely around, waved a sooty hand in a gesture of dismissal. "Let him go. The boy started it and you give 'em a free hand to fight it out. I'm fer law and order. Take 'im away and I'll settle with Tom Shaner." His glance roved around the crowd. "He's been actin' too brash around here lately, anyway. The case is closed agin young Bennett, Mr. Whitmore."

"I ain't so damned sure he's closed his case against you fellers, though," Jim Whitmore said grimly, and slid his gun into its holster. "Bring 'im along, boys. Let's git goin'!"

For the second time in the last twenty-four hours, Weary Willie rode double, steadying Chip Bennett in the saddle. Only this time Chip did not know about it and so did not object.

9. "The Flying U's Back of You"

IN THE HOT AFTERNOON, PUFFY BLUE THUNDERHEADS rolled muttering along the horizon where it merged with the Rockies whenever the trail drive crept across high ground. Within the slow-moving herd the leg-weary calves bawled peevishly for their mothers that outwalked them, and the cows bawled back at them, warning their offspring to come along and mind what they were doing, or they'd be supper for the wolves that liked nothing better than fresh veal. Tricky gusts of wind whipped the gray canopy hanging sluggishly over the herd; shook and lifted it, hurled it viciously upon the ground.

At such times the cowboys, riding slack in their saddles, weight all on one stirrup and swinging the other foot to ease cramped muscles, swore and spat dirt from throats dried with yelling at the stragglers.

"*Hie!* Git back there, you wall-eyed this-that-and-the-other, 'fore I bounce a coupla rocks off'n your ribs! *Hie-ah-h!*"

From Jim Whitmore, riding point, his tall gray horse keeping pace with the huge white ox that led the herd, back to Weary Willie, eating dust and bringing up the drag, every man on the drive was thinking of the same thing. They were thinking of Wane Bennett and his kid brother Chip; thinking it was a damned rotten deal, getting a jolt like that handed out without warning—and him just outa school, as they guessed from certain little earmarks that indicated a refining influence not yet forgotten. Pretty damned tough on the kid. Nothing wrong with his nerve, though, piling into Shaner like that— well, going alone after his gun, for that matter—on top of what had happened just last night. Jumped on the most dangerous man in the country, if you believed all you heard; the man they said was back of Dave Burch and his Vigilantes; the man that knew exactly what had happened to Wane Bennett last fall.

But up in the bed wagon several miles now ahead of the drive, Chip Bennett was not thinking of his nerve in tackling Shaner. Ted Culver was thinking of it, and driving his four horses as quietly as was humanly possible, planning in great detail what he would like to do to Shaner. In the mess wagon just ahead, the Dutch cook Patsy planned how he would, right away when he camped, cut more nice thick slices of beef for the boy's face. Big enough to cover all the bruises. He meditated too upon brown paper soaked in vinegar. They said that was good to take out the soreness. And he would make nice beef broth for the boy. As for Happy Jack, the horse wrangler, leading the entire drive with the remuda, he was gloomily foreseeing dire trouble to come of that fight.

Chip didn't care what the future held for him, what any one put on his face, what the cook fed him. He had only the haziest recollection of that fight, but like a buzzing mosquito the thought tormented him intermittently that he hadn't killed Shaner with his hands, hadn't smashed him, choked him, beaten him, torn him limb from limb, as he had set out to do. Sometimes he couldn't remember why he was going to kill Shaner with his hands. At other times he must listen to the wagon wheels chuckle and chatter, "We hung—your broth—er Wane—we hung—your broth—er Wane—" and he could not figure out what they meant by it, or who had hung his brother Wane; or, mercifully at such times, just who his brother Wane might be.

Part of the time he could smell old sprouting potatoes and he thought he was back in the cellar. Why, he did not know, but he hated to be there and wished Wane would let him out. But mostly he was talking to Goldilocks, and for a long stretch, while the wagon rolled over level ground, he imagined that he was drawing a picture of Julie Lang just as she had looked standing on that rock, with her skirts held up at one side, watching that rattlesnake coiled in the grass. He'd put in the snake with its ugly head lifted, ready to strike. There was something symbolical about that snake coiled at Goldilock's feet, but he couldn't think what it symbolized. Something about treachery, but that couldn't mean Goldilocks.

That night in the crowded bed tent the Flying U boys did not talk at all. Beds were unrolled in complete silence, and in silence men crawled into them. Had it not rained torrents, they would have slept outside and let Chip have the tent to himself—except that Weary Willie stuck close beside him, watching. Weary was not called for night guard that night, though three men instead of two were kept circling the herd because of the storm.

Face swathed in raw beef, Chip lay that night and heard the fiends of hell whisper and jibe, their voices the steady beat of rain on the taut canvas roof. He heard the swish and rattle of wet slickers when guard was changed and those relieved came in and groped in the dark to their blankets. He heard the stamp of night horses, the rattle of stirrups as they moved restlessly, turning rumps to the storm.

They thought he was asleep. He wanted them to think so. He wished the ache in his punished young body were greater, so that it might hammer down the agony of thought; that it might beat into silence that inner cry of "Wane! Wane! Oh, God, Wane!"

It was Weary who lifted his head next morning, held the cup of black coffee carefully against the least injured side of his battered mouth, coaxed him to drink; who afterwards gave him a soup of some kind that Patsy had taken the time and trouble to make, even though it was a rainy morning when camp must be broken and moved. And it was Weary who helped Chip on with his clothes, pulled on his boots for him, bound on fresh slices of beef. "How ya comin', Chip?"

"All right."

"Bet yer bottom dollar you're all right. If you ain't,

we aim to make it right. Best accommodations. Sleepin' car, and no extra fare."

Chip did not answer that. Weary did not expect him to. That day in the bed wagon he slept so heavily that Weary did not attempt to waken him at noon. And the drive went on, crossing creeks swollen with the rain, climbing long slopes of slippery clay, toiling across gumbo flats. On the high spring seat of the bed wagon Ted Culver sat and handled his four horses as best he could, without yelling certain choice objurgations invented by himself on the trail.

Late that afternoon they drove down a long, steep hill, turned sharply away from the Whoop-up Trail and went bumping up a long and fairly wide creek bottom. Chip awoke to the splash of the four horses going through a stream, and for the first time since the fight he thought of little Silver. A worrying thought that brought him to his elbow, clawing bandages away from his sore mouth.

"Hunh?" Ted Culver, who had herded horses all night, turned a startled red-lidded glance back over his shoulder. Chip repeated his question, not very definitely but as well as he could.

"Hunh? The colts? You mean how're they makin' out? Why, fine. Just fine. Say, that geldin's a high stepper, all right! Can't keep 'im nowheres. Just about rules the roost a'ready. Little feller's no slouch, either. Anyway, you needn't worry no more about them colts—er nothin' else, fer as that goes. Pullin' into the home ranch now—and boy, am I glad! No more night hawkin' for yours truly. Them cayuses goes in the pasture till fall round-up. You bet!" He swung forward again, yelled at the leaders a blistering epithet that lacked much of its venom because of the exuberance of his tone.

Chip pulled the fever-tainted meat from his face and threw it overboard, bandages and all. Painfully he pulled himself up until he was half-sitting, leaning against a bed roll, and through empurpled lids stared past the driver. Grassy hillsides with ledgy outcroppings of dark sandstone shut him in, wide meadowland lying lush and green between the coulee walls. Green branches of cottonwood scraped wagon top as they passed, willow bushes drubbed along wheel spokes. From the highest tree tops bird songs drifted down. He mumbled a question that brought Ted Culver's face eagerly around to him.

"Hunh? Are the horses here, y' say? Sure! In the pasture—upper end of the coulee. Happy musta got in an hour ago, maybe more. We throwed a fence across the coulee, up above the cabins." He glanced forward, called his leaders a name, pulled them a little more to the right and looked back. "Ain't fur. I'll drive on up there and give yuh a look." And he chirped to the team.

Not a word about the fight. Not a word about Wane. Ignorant, by all the laws of culture uncouth—even though he might be dashingly picturesque in the saddle—but with that innate fineness which knows how to give comfort unobtrusively and without speech. He drove to the pasture gate, waving a negligent hand to the staring cook and wrangler as he went by the cabins and corrals. He swung his four horses expertly and beckoned with a finger.

"If you can git up here on the seat, Chip, I'll show yuh them colts of yourn." He hitched along to make room, but carefully refrained from offering any assistance. "See 'em over there by the crick? Sure are dandies, all right. Can't see the little feller very good. He's over behind his mother, gittin' his dinner. Lord, how that little bugger can eat! Goin' to make a jim-dandy one of these days."

He waited another full minute before he tightened the reins and kicked off the brake. "Foxy enough to know where the best grass is, along that creek bank," he remarked, with just the right shade of lazy approval. "That geldin's fillin' his belly on Johnny-jump-ups and buttercups. They'll git fat as pigs, all of 'em. Wouldn't mind ownin' that saddle horse of yourn, myself. Bet he's easy-gaited as a rockin'-chair."

"Sure is," Chip agreed mushily, his gaze lingering.

"Yep, that's a fine little bunch of horseflesh," praised Ted, and shut up suddenly, fearing he had overdone it a little.

The four horses trotted down across the springy green sod and pulled up with something of a flourish before the low log building that was evidently the living quarters of the outfit. The cook and horse wrangler, unloading the mess wagon at a second cabin, looked at them with interest, but even Happy Jack, a big and gawky youth with flaming red hair, had the good sense to make no comment.

It was sundown when the riders came trooping down the hill to the north, their faces a mask of trail dust, empty stomachs clamoring for food. And they too made no comment, accepted young Chip Bennett as a matter of course, and did their talking well out of earshot of the subject of their conjectures. Only Weary Willie felt himself privileged to mention the fight to Chip, and even he did not dare more than a discussion of remedies until the need of them was past.

Then, one Sunday afternoon when they were up in the pasture, looking at the colts, Weary broached a ticklish subject. Without warning. "Yuh know, Chip, I think Shaner lied; what he said t' you that time."

Chip held the currycomb poised over Silvia's shining rump. The mask of stoicism dropped over his face, but through it his eyes were probing daggers, terribly alive and insistent. "Lied? In what way?"

Weary gulped, but it had to come out. "About your brother Wane. If that was the truth, it's sure damn funny none of us fellers ever heard it before. Wane," he hurried on, "worked for the Lazy Ladder. He used to cross the river pretty often—he was sweet on Julie Lang, but I don't know as they ever went together. She was goin' with Milt Cummings; you know, the Lazy Ladder boss. You saw him there at the blacksmith shop."

"Yes—I saw him."

"Milt's a nice fellow, all right; everybody likes Milt. Him and Wane got along fine too. You'd kinda think they'd have it in for each other, both likin' the same girl, that way. But there never was any fuss that I ever heard of. That," Weary explained, "was when I was workin' for the Hobble 0, before I quit and went to work for the Lazy Ladder. Well, all anybody knows is, Wane started for Cow Island one evening last fall. That's the last any one ever saw or heard of him. His horse was found about a mile down below the ford, hung up in the willows. He'd been in the water, all right.

"That looked like Wane had got into some kinda jackpot—got off the ford or something—and drowned. We all hunted both sides of the river, down as far as we could go. There never was a sign or trace of him."

"Shaner—" Chip stopped for a full half-minute.

"I know," Weary said, when the silence grew pronounced. "That kinda floored all of us. Me, I don't believe it. He just said that to get back at you. Shaner's a mean devil. Runs the stable there. That crack he made about Wane Bennett being a horse thief—that was just talk. Wane did get into a little trouble when he first come into the country, about a year ago now. But—"

"What trouble?"

"Well, he come up with a bunch of horses; there was six men in the drive. Two was hard customers, accordin' to all accounts—and the Vigilantes got after 'em. Seems most of the horses was stole. Burch and his bunch rounded up all the men and they had a trial. Public, all accordin' to Hoyle. Your brother and another feller proved they was just hired for the drive and didn't know a thing about the horses, or any scaly business. The rest backed 'em up in it, said they was hired after the drive started."

"I heard of Wane down in Wyoming. He was coming up with a bunch of horses." Chip's voice was flat, expressionless.

"Yeah. Well, they turned Wane and this other feller loose. Wane went to work for the Lazy Ladder. The other feller left the country. So that," Weary finished with a relieved sigh, "is all there is to what Shaner made his brag about. Far as anybody knows, anyway. They hung the other four, all right." Weary's voice dropped. "I seen the bodies before they was cut down. I don't ever want to see no more, I tell yuh those. So I know for a fact your brother wasn't in that bunch. And hell, he was punchin' cattle for Milt all summer after that happened, comin' and goin', and Burch and his Vigilantes never givin' him a look, even."

"Thanks, Weary," Chip said after a long pause. His face was turned away.

"I just thought I oughta tell yuh. Wane's dead, but you don't have to go on thinking—that. He drownded, and they say that's about the easiest way there is to go." And he added, with an awkward, boyish attempt at comfort, "You don't want to feel too bad about it, Chip. We all got to go sometime. I'd just as soon go down the river as any other way."

Chip's long, artist fingers combed Silvia's glistening mane. His wide hat brim hid his face. "Wane was all I had left," he said, after a long silence. "There were just us two, after Mother went. Now—" He bit his lip for control "—all I've got is these horses."

Weary blinked, jerked his hat brim savagely over his eyes, laid his hand on Chip's bowed shoulder and let it slide off. "Aw, yuh don't want to feel that way about it," he said gruffly. "Of course, I don't claim to be much, but I guess I oughta be pretty near as good a friend as a horse. And you've got the Flying U." He turned and walked rapidly away, winking very fast and swallowing lumps in his throat. Behind him Chip stood with his arms around Silvia's neck, his face bowed down against her sleek warm shoulder.

10. The Mystery of Wane

HOT DAYS, COOL NIGHTS, FIERCE AND SUDDEN STORMS thundering up from the southwest; long days in the saddle, riding the windswept prairies, pushing the new cattle back upon their range; days when bruises healed and the loneliness of fresh bereavement dulled and insensibly merged into fresh interests, finding new ties for comfort. Which means that young Chip Bennett presently found himself too busy to brood over his troubles very much. It means that the rollicking young cowboys who made up the Flying U personnel unconsciously played an important part in the cure.

J. G. Whitmore hired young fellows to do his work—and masked a fatherly interest by constant grumbling over their coltish performances. But the older men were likely to be hard to handle. If they had been in the West long enough to gain experience, they usually had unsavory records and were not too loyal. At least, that was his theory. So beardless boys did his work for the most part, and he must have been satisfied with the way they did it. At least, he never fired one of them, in spite of the fact that he was constantly threatening to do it. Save himself and Patsy the cook, not a man in the outfit was over thirty; most of them were nearer twenty and full of devilment. Good medicine for Chip, who was in danger of growing too hard and bitter for his years; or for any years, for that matter.

So, that being his present environment, it came quite naturally that the bunk house should be decorated in the next month with cleverly grotesque pictures of certain high lights on the ranch. Facing the door, an elaborately detailed pencil sketch of Happy Jack, who never in the world would become a real rider, soaring high over the back of a terribly contorted bronk. Spurred heels aimed at the zenith, arms outspread, hat going one way and tobacco the other, the likeness was nevertheless star-tling and the caption was, "Happy Dismounts." Chip spent an entire Sunday afternoon drawing that picture, and an entire week convincing Happy Jack that it was on the wall to stay. In that length of time there were other pictures portraying the downfall of other riders—it being the time when horse-breaking was the work to be done. There was one of Chip himself, vividly illus-trating his general impression of how he must have looked to the rest of them during a brief and painful flight into a clump of prickly pear. And since his own mishap looked funnier than any of the others, even Happy Jack grinned finally when he looked at the col-lection and let his own picture stay.

There was one picture they never glimpsed; not even Weary. It was not a large picture and Chip carried it secretly in his coat pocket and gave it little painstaking touches whenever he had a minute alone—which was not often. It was, as you may already have guessed, a picture of Julie Lang, standing on a low flat rock with her skirt held up at the sides displaying a neat ankle, and a snake was coiled and hissing at her, just out of reach.

Chip knew what the symbolic meaning was, now. The snake represented Milt Cummings, for whom he had conceived a violent dislike. Milt Cummings broke bargains and expected the other fellow to keep them, even when the other fellow was a girl. Milt Cummings had tried to take Wane's girl away from him (as Chip interpreted what Weary had told him). No doubt about it, Milt Cummings was the rattlesnake coiled in Goldilocks' path. Chip wished he could label that snake; but that was too raw, of course. He'd have to leave that for Goldilocks to see for herself.

He didn't believe she liked Milt Cummings much, anyway. He wished she hadn't asked Milt to talk Burch out of hanging him. At first that had worried him, but now he saw it in a new light. She hadn't much time, and she was ready to do anything on earth to save him. She'd even ask a favor of Milt Cummings.

Penciling the diamond shadings on the snake's back, that thought softened his lips into a dreamy half smile. She must have liked him right from the start. Not the way he liked her, of course, but enough to show she realized, the same as he did, that it was fate that brought them together. She called him *dear*—because it was in her mind, and when she was worried about him, the word slipped out before she realized what she was saying. Chip cherished that memory, and the picture she had made, standing there calling all those men brutes because they didn't stop the fight.

He had been just about crazy, wanting to smash Shaner—beat him into the ground as he would a snake, for what he had said—but he wasn't so crazy he wouldn't always remember his little Goldilocks standing there, ready to fight for him. It always made his heart pound, just thinking about it. That, he thought exultantly, that certainly must have been a hard pill for Milt Cummings to swallow! Seeing Julie Lang, modest as she was, walk right into that fight and go after Shaner with her fists. Like a kitten tackling a bulldog; or a canary fighting a hawk.

He supposed she was wondering why he never had gone to see her again. One letter he had written and sent down by a freighter he happened to meet. He had explained that he was pretty busy helping break horses and range herding those cattle they brought up, and he had tried to thank her for what she had done. He'd come as soon as he could, he said. But now he was tormented with the thought that maybe she never saw that letter. Maybe the freighter got drunk and forgot to give it to her, and took it on down to Billings or wherever he was headed for. Maybe—and Chip turned hot and cold and prickly when he thought of it—maybe he opened the letter and read it. The dirty skunk!

So none of the Flying U boys ever so much as glimpsed that exquisite study of Julie Lang which Chip was carrying hidden in his pocket, or guessed what was going on behind those steady brown eyes.

His bitterness toward Shaner they knew, without having to be told. They also knew that it had hit him pretty hard to come all the way up from Denver to find his brother, only to discover that he had been dead for months. Pretty damned tough, they called it, and when he withdrew behind his wall of silence, they let him alone, taking it for granted that he was thinking of Wane. Sometimes he was, but youth is nothing if not resilient, and lately his thoughts had been with Julie Lang more often than the Flying U boys would have believed.

Among themselves, they wondered whether Chip would feel like going to the big "doings" Lang was giving on the Fourth. Being all broken up over losing his brother, they thought maybe Chip would stay home. Still, they didn't know. He had acted lately like he was kinda getting over it a little; the way he'd been deviling the bunch with all those pictures the last week or two and wrassling around with the boys evenings, it looked like he'd about got his troubles whipped. They sure hoped so. They'd like to see him ride in there and show Shaner he didn't give a damn.

An air of pleased excitement pervaded the Flying U ranch that last Sunday before the Fourth. Private horses were being curried and brushed until they shone like satin. Their tails were trimmed and cleaned, tightly braided, looped and tied, so they would be nice and crinkly when the occasion arrived for showing off. Slim, the camp barber, had spent the entire forenoon out on the shady side of the bunk house, cutting hair and trimming the mustaches of those who fancied such adornment.

Down on the creek bank, squatting on their boot heels beneath an old willow tree, Chip and Weary were washing their best shirts and socks and handkerchiefs. Their big hats were pushed back on their heads and a tin can of golden brown soft soap sat between them on the gravelly bank.

"You're goin' along, ain't yuh, Chip?" Weary asked, in as casual a manner as he could contrive.

"Sure, I'm going along." Chip answered him calmly.

"Good. What horse yuh goin' to ride?" Weary dipped three fingers in the brown jelly and rubbed the soap carefully into a sweat-stained collar. When he glanced up from the work, his eyes matched the underside of the collar where the blue had not faded. "Silvia?" he hinted, still artfully casual.

"No; Mike, I guess. He's the best for what I intend to do."

With the back of his hand Weary slapped a mosquito just taking a first bite on his forehead where the skin was white and tender. "If you're goin' to get in the horse racing, you oughta ride that mare down," he suggested hopefully. "I bet she could clean up the whole works, even if she has got a suckin' colt."

"I'll tell a man she could!" Chip grinned and soaped the feet of a pair of socks. "I wouldn't be afraid to run Silvia against any horse in the country. She's faster than greased lightning, far as that goes."

"Mamma!" breathed Weary. "Then you sure oughta ride her. There's a bunch down around Rocky Point I'd like to show a thing or two. Folks are coming from all over. Lang's goin' to spread himself this year. Puttin' in a dance hall—course, you heard all that. Tryin' to make a town of it, I guess. Anyway, there'll be a big doin's, and don't you forget it. Band from the fort to furnish music for the dance—Mamma! Chance to clean up some real money on a race or two. You oughta give us fellers a chance to bet on that mare, Chip." Weary let the shirt float in the lazy current where inch-long minnows tasted it and flipped away, gasping.

"Well, I would, maybe, only the colt would have to go along. I don't want him taggin'. Not where I expect to ride."

"Hunh? Where's that, for gosh sake?" Weary looked at him, startled. "What crazy notion you got now?"

Chip's face subtly hardened. "Nothing crazy about it. I'm going to find out why Wane drowned last fall when the river was low as it ever gets, and he was crossing on that ford he must have known as well as I know the way from here to the mess house. Why, even this spring you can't call it dangerous, Weary. Little Silver swam it, and so did several hundred calves. We never lost a single critter. And Wane was a good swimmer. And his horse got out all right, you said."

"Yeah, that's right," said Weary, weighting the shirt with a rock, so the current would rinse out the soap, and drying his hands on his front so that he could roll a cigarette. "It did look kinda funny, and that's a fact. The supposition among the boys was—" He stopped abruptly and fumbled with his cigarette papers.

"The supposition was that he was drunk. Is that it?"

"Well, yeah. That's about the only way it *could* of happened."

Chip drew a long breath, lips pressed tight. "Did you ever see my brother drunk?" He took another sharp breath. "On the square, Weary. Never mind hurting my feelings—it's the facts I'm trying to get at. Did you?"

"No-o-no, I never did. But then," Weary added honestly, "I never was around where he was, hardly."

"Did you ever hear any one say they saw him drunk?"

"Never did. Never heard a hell of a lot about him, Chip—not after that big session with the Vigilantes. Seemed to be a pretty nice, quiet fellow; far as I ever heard."

Chip rolled himself a cigarette, trying for a calm consideration of the subject. He felt in his pocket for a match but forgot to light it. He looked at Weary, looked away again. "Wane wasn't the drinking type," he said. "About as much as I am, and a glass of beer on a hot day is about my limit. I don't believe it was that. I can't get it out of my head there's something covered up. If there wasn't, if it was just a straight accident, why would Shaner make that remark to me?"

"Him?" Weary exhaled a mouthful of smoke. "That old rip would say anything if he thought it would hurt a man."

Chip stared down at the blue shirt gently waving in the creek, but what he saw was Wane fording the Missouri in the dark. The picture was quite clear and unalarming. He shook his head in a baffled sort of way. "Wane must have known every inch of that ford. If he got off it in the dark—but his horse knew it as well as he did; better, maybe. He wouldn't get off the ford. But if he did—hell, Wane was no tenderfoot."

Weary took his cigarette from his mouth, looked at it, flicked off the ash. "Yeah, I've heard other folks say the same thing," he said softly.

"Who?" Chip's gaze was upon him, trying to read the answer before it was spoken.

"Why—several. I was workin' for the Hobble O when it happened. The boys at the ranch talked about it some. So did the Lazy Ladder boys. They all thought it was kinda funny—unless he was drunk or something."

"But nobody said he was drunk, did they? Nobody, like Lang or the bartender, whoever he is—no one like that, who would be supposed to know?"

"I never heard 'em. There was another bunch of hard customers caught and—you know what—right about then. The talk about your brother kinda died down in a day or two." Weary turned and looked soberly at him. "I wisht you could try and forget about it, Chip. There's no way you can find out about it now. If somebody framed that accident, it looks to me like they made it stick. Put it outa your mind, can't yuh?"

"No." Chip spoke more harshly than he intended. "There's another thing, Weary. What became of all Wane's things; horses, saddle and bridle, clothes, bed— all that stuff? He started out with as good an outfit as I've got, only he just had the two horses."

"Yeah, I remember when they turned him loose at Cow Island he was riding a good-looking bay and leading a pack horse. Black, I think it was. And now I think of it, they both carried the reversed EB brand."

"Dude—that's the sorrel—and Pegleg was the pack horse's name. What became of them? The horse he rode that night was found all right, you said."

Weary took a long pull at his cigarette and cast the stub into a sunny pool where the minnows immediately swarmed up to investigate it before it sank. He watched them absently, then turned his head and looked at Chip, who was staring unseeingly at the barren bluff opposite them. "Milt must have the horses down at the Lazy Ladder. I s'pose Wane's stuff is all there too. A course he'd hold it till some one come along that had a right to claim it. I never happened to see the horses that I know of—I s'pose they're runnin' out. All you got to do, Chip, is ask him about it. I don't know what you got against Milt. He sure is a fine fellow. Anybody'd tell yuh that."

"Yes? Well, I don't care to be beholden to him for taking care of my brother's horses and outfit, so I'll just ask him to turn them over to me. I guess I can prove by J.G. that I've got a right."

Weary gave him an odd look. "Mamma! You carry the proof right under your hat, far as that goes. If you was his age, you'd be his twin, almost. Milt knows you're Wane's brother, all right."

11. Jim Whitmore's Happy Family

COW ISLAND WAS CELEBRATING THE FOURTH. RAUCOUS yelling, the barking of six-shooters fired into the air, the staccato popping of firecrackers made patriotic uproar as the Flying U boys came galloping down to the ford. Dave Burch's two anvils, set one upon the other with plenty of gunpowder between and fired by the simple method of applying the red-hot end of a long iron rod to the powder trail laid for that purpose, boomed like a cannon across the river, borne by the warm breeze that rippled the water. And at the sound of it, the horses snorted and threw up their heads, lifting their knees in high prancing steps, as they stared toward the noise.

"My gosh! We can't ride these cayuses into that—unless we want to put in our day in the saddle learning 'em manners," Cal Emmett complained. "I don't know about you fellows, but this here buzzard head of mine sure won't stand for that racket. Not for one holy minute."

"What d' yuh think we are, anyway?" Jack Bates demanded. "Think we're goin' to walk in like a bunch of sheep-herders? Me, I'm goin' to ride right up to the front door. To hell with what my horse thinks about it. I'm ridin' him, ain't I?"

"You're settin' in the saddle with your legs hangin' down," Cal admitted with a grin. "A person couldn't hardly call it *ridin'* though."

"You won't even be doin' that much when we get up there," Jack retorted. "You keep your eye peeled for Cal," he called over his shoulder at Chip, who was riding behind him. "I'm goin' to want a pitcher of him when they shoot off that anvil alongside that broomtail of his."

"It's liable to be a group picture," Chip answered him. "A correct imitation of shooting stars." But he did not smile when he said it. It was his first sight of the river since Weary had told him of Wane's tragic end there, and he was finding it difficult to keep his thoughts off the subject.

His words started argument, however, and before they reached the south bank, they were betting on who could ride closest to the blacksmith shop without getting "piled." So they dismounted on the bank and tightened cinches, dented hat crowns to please their vanity and catch the glances of the girls, and otherwise made ready for an effective arrival. Turk Bowles, the ferryman, doubly afflicted with a "tied" tongue and a harelip, gobbled pleasantries to which they replied at random, since no one had the time to decipher his speech. And they mounted and rode decorously toward the noise.

The flat where freight outfits were accustomed to camp was thickly sprinkled with vehicles of all descriptions, the teams unhitched and tied to the wheels or to convenient trees, munching hay thrown down in piles on the ground. At each fresh clamor in the settlement, the harness rattled on their backs as they jumped and snorted. Nervous saddle horses were there also; dozens of them tied to trees and wincing at the noise.

A lanky young man whose trousers hung loose around his bony frame stepped out into the road and waved his arms in a signal to halt. "Better not ride yer hosses no furder 'n this," he advised importantly. "Too blame much shootin' goin' on up there. Shaner's stable an' c'rel's full up, an' he says evbody's got t' tie their hosses down here outa the way—" He jumped back out of danger. "Hey! You can't ride your hosses up there!" he shouted excitedly.

But the Flying U boys had bets to settle and they could ride their horses where they pleased. In a whirlwind of dust they charged past him and went whooping up the trail, shooting as they rode. When it came to noise, they tacitly decided that they could do quite a bit themselves.

Half-grown boys pressing close to the exciting circle around the door of the blacksmith shop scattered precipitately as the eight riders thundered up. Two men came running out with the heated rod, thrust it upon the thin line of powder and ducked back. With the roar that followed, eight horses went into action. The Flying U boys holstered their guns and rode the cyclones out, yelling and yipping to show their scorn of Shaner and his orders.

There were casualties. Happy Jack rooted his red face in the dust, and the young man called Penny fell flat on his back and came near being stepped on by Weary's gyrating animal. Chip's horse Mike contented himself with two or three crow hops, so Chip was free to catch the two riderless horses and bring them to their owners; and by that time the show was over. Turning their backs upon Shaner, they rode across to Lang's place and dismounted at the hitch rail, settled their hats upon their heads and walked up the steps together.

From the doorway of the saloon Barr Lang himself gave a shout of welcome. "Jim Whitmore's Happy Family!" he chortled to those around him. "J.G. raises 'em by hand on wolf meat and rattlesnake oil and they run in packs, like you seen 'em just now. Take 'em or leave 'em—you can't break the set!" He gave a bellowing laugh at his own crude wit. "H' are yuh, boys? Keg uh beer there, just outa the ice house. Drink hearty!"

"Happy Family, hunh? That's a good one!" A Lazy Ladder man laughed and pushed out past Lang, "Oh, hello, Weary," he added, as his glance went around the group. "How yuh comin'?"

"On the dead run, Spike," Weary grinned back at him and reached for a beer mug. "How's tricks?"

Others crowded in around the keg, which lay on its side on a convenient trestle built for the purpose. Its spigot never lacked fingers to turn it, and a dozen mugs stood on a near-by table, a tub of water beside them for quick washing, if a man happened to be finicky.

Barr Lang was a diplomat. He waited until their thirst was temporarily quenched and tactfully broached the subject of Fourth of July rules. "Yuh don't want to spoil your appetites, boys," he said deprecatingly. "Don't go buyin' bologny an' crackers, or figure on the dinin' room bein' open. It ain't, and it won't be till t'night. The women folks is engineerin' a picnic back up here in the grove. We got a place all cleared out, swings for the little shavers—tables an' benches to set on. After dinner they'll be speeches and singin'. We've got a platform, and the boys packed our organ up there. No flies on this Fourth!"

He cleared his throat gustily, saw Shaner heading over that way from the stable, and continued more hurriedly. "After the doin's in the grove, boys, they'll be races an' sports out here in the street. An' the kids swarmin' all over the place with their firecrackers—so it might be a good idee, boys, to take your horses down with the rest and tie 'em up. Soon as I can git my hands on that damn garter snake of a Hec Grimes, I'll have a jag uh hay hauled down there for 'em. Some folks here from Rocky Point with a slather of young ones, an' I promised the women I'd kinda keep the street clear uh horses, so their brats wouldn't get their heads kicked off 'em. You know how it is," he apologized, making an unobtrusive sign to Shaner. "I got t' stand in with all of 'em."

"Why, sure!" cried Shorty, who was the oldest of the lot and usually the boss in Jim Whitmore's absence. "We only come up here to settle a bet or two—"

"And to show Tom Shaner where to head in at," Jack Bates cut in remindingly. "Don't overlook that, Shorty."

"Yeah. Hec tried to hold us up down there in the flat; told us Shaner wouldn't let us ride our horses into town," Cal Emmett explained.

"And we ain't takin' orders from that old billy goat, now nor no time," Penny further elucidated.

Barr Lang saw that Shaner had heeded his signal and was going back to the stable, and he gave his great bellowing laugh. "What'd I tell yuh?" he asked the crowd around him. "Didn't I tell yuh Jim Whitmore raises 'em on wolf meat—"

"And we sure know how to howl!" Ted Culver interrupted him shortly. "Come on, boys. This is getting too damn personal around here to suit me." He turned on his heel and started for his horse.

"Now, now, don't go off mad," Lang protested, still chuckling.

"We ain't mad," Weary threw over his shoulder, as they headed for the hitch rail. "We're happy as hell. Ain't we, boys?"

"Just like he said; one happy family of he-wolves on the prowl," Cal agreed in a loud voice, so that all might hear. Whereupon they mounted and spurred straight across the wide road toward Tom Shaner, who length-ened his stride perceptibly when he heard the tumult behind him. Shooting, yelling, howling in very bad imi-tation of wolves, they chased him to the stable door, swerved sharply away and swept down past the black-smith shop, so close to the anvils that the two men coming out with their freshly heated iron rod dropped it and ducked back inside; which pleased the Flying U boys immensely.

A tow-headed boy threw a lighted firecracker in front of them and then dug bare toes in the sand, running for his life, scared at what he had done but ardently hoping to see some one bucked off.

He was disappointed. The cracker fizzed out and was mashed beneath a hoof that did not know it was there. The howling Flying U wolves went thundering down to the camp ground, their departure punctuated—but not speeded—by the tardy roar of the anvils behind them.

12. Chip Doesn't Like Picnics

ON THE WHOLE, THE NEWLY CHRISTENED HAPPY FAMILY felt fairly well satisfied with their brief but pointed dec-laration of independence. While they tied their horses to trees, loosened cinches and removed the bridles, hanging them over the saddle-horns so that horses might eat in comfort, if that string bean of a Hec ever brought the hay, they voiced freely their opinion of the celebration as far as it had gone.

Cow Island, they said, was sure getting tony, keeping horses off the roadway it called a street. Didn't Lang and Shaner know that every darned kid in the country was used to horses? How did they suppose those brats kept their heads from getting kicked off at home? There wasn't one in the country, hardly, that would be fool enough to walk up behind a strange bronk.

Chip said nothing at all. He had ridden with the boys, but in silence. He didn't want Goldilocks to think he was drunk, if she should happen to be looking out of the window and saw him. No use giving her the idea he was a rowdy and didn't know any better.

While he made Mike comfortable with a tree to himself and an armful of hay purloined from under the very nose of a broad-hipped old mare nodding and switching at flies beside a farm wagon, he considered ways and means of seeing Julie alone. He wondered if she had seen him yet. If she knew he was in town, she would maybe keep an eye out for him. It would be easier if she did a little planning herself and kind of edged away from the crowd when she saw him coming, he thought, as he removed his chaps and spurs and hung them on the saddle, dusted himself off with his hands and otherwise prepared to plunge into the social whirl of Cow Island. He was ready to go when the boys discovered how simply he had provided a meal for Mike and forthwith went hunting hay piles for their own horses.

It was the opportunity Chip had hoped for. Unobserved, he walked off and left them, and with his cigarette in his lips to give him nonchalance strolled up past the kitchen of the Lang House as if that were the most natural path in the world to take. With a sulky indifference calculated to hide his embarrassment, he glanced in at the open door, and in ten seconds took a mental inventory of the occupants. Aunt Amanda was there, all dressed up and talking to beat four of a kind; four other women were also talking and seeming not to mind because no one listened. But there was no Goldilocks in sight.

Secretly relieved because he would not have to face the eye and tongue of Aunt Amanda, he went on to the grove, whence came squeals and shrill chatter of children at play. Through the trees he had caught the flutter of blue among the women's dresses glimpsed in the distance as they flitted about long tables, and with a set scowl on his face—again to hide his inward torment—he walked steadily toward them.

Plucking Julie out of that swarm was going to be a devil of a job. He almost lost his nerve and turned back. Perhaps he would have done so if a stout, tightly corseted woman with a fresh, good-natured face had not come hurrying toward him.

"Beg pardon," Chip said earnestly, tipping his big hat as she came up. "I was looking for Will Davidson—friend of mine. Is—"

"Don't know him. He isn't here, for if he was, I'd have grabbed him long ago to see what ails that pesky fire." Her smile was the friendly, anxious smile of a distracted hostess who wants to serve dinner but can't get the gravy to bubble. She caught Chip by the elbow and held to it firmly, waving her other hand to some one in the grove. "I said I'd bring a man if I had to hog-tie him and drag him in by the heels, and I've got one," she cried, in a pleasant shout meant to carry over distance.

To Chip she explained further, as she hurried him forward. "We've got-to have a fire for the coffee. They're getting it started down at the house to save time, but they'll bring it up pretty quick—two wash boilers full. And them pesky boys brought in green alder and then ducked out of here, like they'd stirred up a hornets' nest. The fire's smoked till the girls all look as if they'd been bawling their eyes out because their best fellow'd gone back on 'em. You see what you can do. What we want is a good bed of coals but it's a cinch we'll never get 'em as things stand now."

A blurred panorama of strange women swam before Chip's eyes. Little rushing sentences, giggles, meaningless exclamations fused into unintelligible cadence not unlike running water falling over rocks. And in the midst of it all a slim little figure in ruffled blue lawn was coming toward him, blue eyes widened with a startled look, mouth giving that look the lie by smiling. The glow in his own eyes answered the smile as he went toward her.

"I've corralled some one to fix that fire," his captor was saying exultantly. "You girls put him to work. I don't know what his name is—but I s'pose he's got one."

Giggles answered that. Julie Lang, who might have introduced him properly, turned away to rescue her little dog Tiny from possible annihilation by a tolerant shepherd with bushy tail wagging violently as he sniffed and panted, red tongue draped over his teeth.

Two bold-eyed young women closed in upon Chip, laughing at nothing at all. They led him away toward a feebly smoking pile of wood, but over the shoulder of one he saw, or thought he saw, a promise in Julie's eyes. And for the moment he was content.

But not for long. Afterward that day remained in Chip's memory as a nightmare too disagreeably vivid to forget, but with the details a confused muddle of incidents. He seemed to have spent hours nursing that damnable fire, with strange girls milling around him. He was still there a captive while the crowd ate, and he would bet that, out of two wash boilers of coffee, he dipped at least four barrels, filling dinky little pitchers in the hands of giggling volunteer waitresses.

True, Julie was one of them. But she might have been a perfect stranger, for all the good it did him. When she stood with her pitcher and he could catch her eye, she smiled, but so did every other girl who came near him. True, she brought him a great wedge of chocolate cake on her second trip, but other girls brought sandwiches for him to eat while he dipped and poured; and pie which he must hold and eat from his left hand; and pickles which they invited him to bite while they obligingly held the thing for him.

Not once did Julie stand alone beside him. Not once did she speak two words for his ears alone. And when the coffee was down to the soggy bags of grounds, and the tables looked as though a herd of cattle had fed there, the first young women attempted to lead him over to the platform, where Dave Burch in a black frock coat too tight for him was preparing to read the Declaration of Independence. Chip went far enough to see Julie's yellow head behind the organ, and Milt Cummings sitting there beside her, with three or four other men and a couple of girls. He even waited until they were halfway through "America," Milt Cumming's turning Julie's music and singing tenor.

That was too much for Chip. He didn't know where the other boys were, but as far as he was concerned, he had had enough. And enough, he told himself savagely, was a damn plenty. "America" was a dinky little short piece, anyway and it was probably all on one page. Milt Cummings might make a bluff at turning the page, but he couldn't fool Chip. He made Chip sick, stalling that way, just wanting to show off. Making a grand-stand play—and she was silly enough to let Milt get away with it.

With a curl of his lip to show the world his scorn of the whole sickening performance, Chip turned and walked down behind the seated crowd and out of the grove, heedless of Weary's insistent beckoning gestures from the outermost fringe of spectators. In his present mood he hated every one; himself, Julie Lang, even Weary and Cal and the rest of them. If they hadn't any more brains than to sit and goggle at that big ape, let them stay, but he'd be damned if he was going to.

The short cut he took carried him down past the cellar of gruesome memory. Curiosity impelled him to pause and inspect his prison, but not for long. In spite of himself, he shuddered as he saw the stout, slanting door with its great handmade hinges and hasp, no doubt hammered out on Dave Burch's anvil. The big padlock, the bar made of two logs joined with slabs and weighted with rocks, ready to be lifted across the door as an extra precaution against escape—no wonder Julie had refused any attempt to help him out that way. The roof, he saw, had been repaired and reinforced with logs, and now there was no ventilator of any kind. But the door lay open, and from the odor of musty vegetables, he guessed that the potato heap was still down there. A horrible hole to throw a man into for his last hours on earth.

Walking fast away from there, he came around the corner of the new addition to the saloon, the dance hall decorated with bunting and ready for the grand opening that night. Not all the celebrants were in the grove, he discovered. A shout of laughter reached him from the open windows of the saloon next door. A man came out and hurried to the hitch rail where a horse was tied.

Chip's eyes followed him and his heart leaped up and stuck in his throat. He could feel the skin on his face shrink and stiffen—the hair on his neck rise as a chill shot up his spine. For the horse standing there within a dozen yards of him was Wane's saddle horse, Dude.

13. "Steer Clear of That Bunch!"

CHIP'S STRICKEN EYES FLASHED INSTINCTIVELY TO THE brand. The reversed EB was still discernible, in spite of the blotchy Window Sash brand burned over it. Just so, the tall, bony sorrel with the sweat-roughened flanks scored by the cruel spurring was instantly recognizable as the once sleek, well-groomed horse of which Wane had been so proud. The light sorrel coat, white stockings to the knees in front, the narrow white blaze down the nose, ending in a diamond point between the large intelligent eyes could not be mistaken, even without that crudely disguised brand.

And there were Wane's bridle and saddle, with no attempt at disguise. The saddle was short-skirted, the rounded corners cut according to Wane's idea. Made to order in Denver, it had been. And Chip himself had drawn the wild-rose design for the saddle maker to follow. Cunningly hidden in leaf and tendril, so that only when it was pointed out could it be seen, Wane's name was stamped in the pattern. Gawain; pronounced in the Bennett household with the accent on the last syllable.

Wane had always hated that name as high-toned or something. When, one day in school, a bigger boy had shown him a picture of a plumed knight called Gawain—Bennett added in lead pencil—Wane had licked three boys in the school yard for trying to stick a feather in his hat and asking him where were his tin pants. After that he had written his name *Wane,* and had achieved permanent black eyes while teaching his world to forget the other. Some boyish grudge had inspired Chip to draw that name into the wild-rose design. And when the saddle was done and he showed the word to Wane, he had been pretty thoroughly trounced by his cowboy brother for the trick.

It could not have been more than a few seconds that he stood motionless, staring, held in the grip of that stark recollection. It seemed that not until this moment, with Wane's horse and saddle there before his eyes, had the loss of his brother come home to him. It was like twisting a knife in his heart when the sorrel threw up its head and gave him a questioning stare, as if asking him why he stood there doing nothing about it. Then the man was in the saddle, had jabbed in his spurs and was off down the road in a whirl of dust.

With a gasp, Chip came to himself, bitterly reproaching himself for his inaction. In spite of that fellow's two guns he should have run out and knocked him down or something. His own gun was down on the saddle, the belt hidden under his chaps. It wasn't polite to wear a gun when you went to see a girl—though he wished now, foolishly, that he had stuck his gun inside his waistband as some of the other boys had done. He could have held the fellow up—

Not until he met Hec Grimes halfway down to the flat did he realize that he was running at top speed. He slowed, halted the listless choreman of Barr Lang. "Who was that fellow on—on the sorrel?" he panted. "Where's he going?"

Hec turned himself deliberately around, gazed down toward the ferry. "Him? Cash Farley. Goin' back to camp, I reckon."

"Come along." Chip whirled Hec by the arm, pulled him along beside him, slowing his stride to a fast walk. "Talk while I throw the saddle on my horse. What camp d' you mean?"

"Big Butch's camp, over across the river some'ers. Say, what's eatin' on yuh? You don't want no truck with Cash Farley."

Chip gave him a quick look. "Why not? Who is he?

Who's Big Butch?"

Hec turned his head on his long thin neck and stared. "Say, you talk like a dawgone pilgrim. Cash Farley's one uh Big Butch's head killers, so I've heard 'em say. And Big Butch, he's about the meanest, killin'est, stealin'est son of a gun they is in the country. That's one bunch the Vigilantes don't dast t' look sideways at, an' don't you forget it!"

They had reached the horses. Chip let go of Hec, snatched his chaps off the saddle and pulled them on in a hurry. Not until he was buckling on his gun belt did he speak again. Then, "What's Cash Farley doing with my brother's horse and saddle?" he demanded.

"Hunh?" Hec looked almost insulted. "How'd yuh s'pose I know?" He gave a short cackling laugh. "I ain't never heard none uh that bunch explain what they're doin' with nothin'," he interpreted his amusement. "That's a good one, that is."

Across Mike's back Chip gave him a sharply impatient glance as he tightened the cinch. "There's nothing so damn funny about it. My brother's dead, and that fellow's got his horse and saddle—"

"Ain't funny to you, ner me either," Hec broke in on him. "But if you was older and knowed more about this country, it wouldn't be nothin' strange. Funny part is you needin' any explanation about it."

Chip bit his lip. "I don't. Not from you, anyway. I guess I'm capable of going to headquarters for any explanation I need. Where's that camp of theirs?"

Hec spat tobacco juice between broken teeth. His pale blue eyes squinted at Chip. "Say, if folks like me knowed where it was, it wouldn't be no hell of a hideout, would it?"

"You must have some idea. Where do you think it is?"

"Oh. Well, that's different," Hec conceded. "I got an idea it's back somewheres in there." He pulled a hand from his pocket and flapped it loosely toward the river. "Ten, fifteen mile, mebby. You ain't goin' t' go huntin' for it, are yuh?"

"And why not?" snapped Chip, slipping the bit into Mike's mouth and the headstall over his ears.

"Well, hell! Ain't I just been *tellin'* yuh?" Hec's Adam's apple jerked up and down. "Ain't I told yuh they're plumb snaky? You take a bunch like that Big Butch gang—that can ride in here any time they damn please, stay as long as they want to and ride out again and Dave Burch nor Shaner nor Barr Lang nor *nobody* darin' to say a word to 'em about their goin's on, why—" He spat again "—you're crazy to think of such a thing." He gave Chip a worried look. "When you go huntin' Big Butch's hideout you're ridin' a one-way trail, boy. You steer clear of that bunch."

"I will—like hell!" gritted Chip, and was in the saddle and gone before Hec could think of any stronger argument against his going.

Halfway to the ford Chip said, "Like hell I'll steer clear!" in a savage mutter that brought Mike's ears tilting backward to hear. The ferry was just swinging in empty to the bank as he rode past, and with a sudden impulse, he reined sharply back to the landing. "You needn't tie up," he called out to Turk Bowles. "Boost

118

'er around here so I can ride on. And you needn't take all day, either!"

Turk grinned and gobbled something about a "High ole hime uh Hourth", which seemed to imply that fellows who forded the river on other days rode the ferry across today by way of celebrating. Chip nodded and let it go at that. Cash Farley had taken the ferry, probably because it was a little quicker and a good deal easier on his horse. Wane's horse. Not for one moment did Chip forget that. Nor did he overlook the fact that Farley was the kind who would save his horse only because he wanted to get more out of him later on. So he must be in a hurry.

Yet to Chip, standing there on the hot planks of the old scow and rubbing Mike's nose to quiet him, it seemed as though they merely swung out into the full current and remained there in one spot, the boat bobbing gently to meet the little waves lapping along its side. He wished he had waded the ford. He would have, except that Cash Farley had ridden the ferry across and he must have had some reason for doing so. He must have found it quicker, even though it felt so slow.

When Mike decided that there was nothing to get excited about and relaxed into a mildly interested posture, Chip pulled his gun from its holster, ejected what shells were empty and replaced them with loaded cartridges. His hand went back to the butt of his carbine hanging in its scabbard on the saddle. He had fired three shots at a couple of wolves, that morning on the way in, and he had no recollection of refilling the magazine. He did so now, breaking open a fresh box of cartridges taken from a saddle pocket.

Turk Bowles watched him curiously, his gaze shifting from the gun to Chip's face bent above it. None of Turk's business, but this cowboy shore did look and act like he was ready for bear. Shore wouldn't be healthy to go pickin' a fuss with him—not the way he looked now. EB horse; Turk scowled, trying to remember what outfit in the country carried that brand . . . shore had seen it somewhere before. . . .

And suddenly, Turk gave a muttered exclamation and walked to the other end of the boat, wagging his head and stealing a glance now and then over his shoulder. Gosh, no wonder he thought the feller had looked kinda familiar! Must be that young catamount they'd dern near hung, a month or so ago; the one that had tried to lick Shaner. Wane Bennett's brother, that's who he was. From a distance Turk eyed him with interest, wondering what was on his chest now. Shore on the prod about something, if looks didn't lie.

Chip never gave Turk a thought. He was a part of the ferry; as such, he tossed the fare back to him, mounted and rode clattering off the boat without a glance or a thought for anything but the marks of Dude's hoofs printed deep in the moist sand before him. Those imprints Mike deepened and blurred with his own galloping feet, as Chip swung him into the Whoop-up trail, a brownish yellow stripe of rutted sand, twisting away into the hills.

In the picnic grove the air had been sultry, filled with high-darting swarms of gnats and the languid hum of mosquitoes. Out here in the full blaze of sunlight a fitful breeze whipped up the dust in little spurts and fanned Chip's face with a furnace blast of heat. He never felt it. He was aware of the wind only because those spirals of dust bothered him a little when they rose out of the trail ahead. Made it hard to tell which small cloud was made by the passing of Cash Farley.

He couldn't be far ahead. Not over a mile, anyway. It wouldn't matter so much if he kept to the trail. Dude was a good fast horse, but Mike was in better condition. . . . Dude sure looked like a string of suckers, all ganted up like that. . . . Looked as if that damned Farley took him out and rode him to a whisper every day or so. A man that would leave spur marks like that on as good a horse as old Dude, ought to be shot. . . . Sure was lucky he'd swiped that bunch of hay for Mike. He was good for a long chase now; in better shape for it than Dude. If Wane knew how his horse was being abused . . .

Chip pulled his thoughts back to the chase, to the storm-breeding weather, to the yellowing hills where the fierce midsummer heat was already ripening the grasses. Wild sunflowers nodding in thick patches along the trail sent their pungent odor into the air as he galloped past. . . . That one dust cloud that stuck to the trail and kept moving right along it; that must be Cash Farley. You'd think he'd be turning off into the hills pretty soon. The longer he stuck to the main road, though, the better. Better going. Another four or five miles like this, and Mike would be crawling up on him. Just what he would do when he did overtake Cash Farley Chip left to the moment when it happened. He was much more concerned with the possibility of losing track of him in the hills.

He very nearly did. He had topped a low ridge with a long gentle slope beyond, tipping down to a rocky gulch with a creek running through. At a point where the low cliffs broke down on either hand to rough boulders and jagged outcroppings, the trail crossed the creek and bore away to the left, toward the river. From the crest of the ridge, Chip could look down the slope to the crossing and on to where the road swung around a high barren butte. Just short of the crossing he caught sight of his quarry, a little more than half a mile away and riding at a gallop. He had gained nearly half the distance between himself and Big Butch's head killer.

Wet to the ears with sweat though he was, Mike held to the terrific pace, ears laid back and hard-muscled legs working like pistons. Without a falter in his stride he swept down into the hollow, out and up on the farther side and on down to the creek; across it in two great splashes and on again, as if he were after a runaway cow.

They had reached the bend around the butte before Chip realized that something was wrong. The fresh imprints of galloping hoofs had ceased altogether in the trail. Somewhere in the last half mile they must have turned aside. By his very eagerness to come up with Farley he had missed him.

He pulled Mike to a stand, studied the trail and the surrounding country, frowning over the puzzle. Cash Farley must have looked back and seen him coming. Chip supposed that a killer would think first of jumping into the brush and waiting until the man behind him had gone by. He'd "dry gulch" the man that chased him; at any rate, he would, if he thought he were being followed. According to all the stories men told, that was the way outlaws worked the game.

While he rolled and lighted a cigarette, Chip studied the technique of "dry gulching." He tried to put himself in Cash Farley's boots and to think as an outlaw would think. So—he'd hunt cover, soon as he saw a man coming after him like that. He'd wait till the fellow came up and see who he was, then use his own judgment about killing him. That was only common horse sense, as Chip saw it.

Well, Farley hadn't shot him out of the saddle as he went past, so it was safe to say he decided that Chip was just some fellow in a hell of a hurry to get somewhere. He didn't know Chip—had never seen him before and wouldn't suspect what Chip's hurry was for. He might be an outlaw, but he was no mind reader; that was a cinch. Even if he stayed where he was and watched for a while, lie—but he wouldn't. He'd go on wherever he was going.

Chip waited a few minutes, pretending to be tightening the cinch. He could see the trail, or most of it, clear back to the ridge. And it was empty. He mounted and rode back slowly, watching the ground under Mike's nose. He was as keen-eyed as any young fellow who lives much in the open and whose business it is to "read signs" and ride where trails are dim. But look as he would, he could see no sign where Farley had left the trail.

Beyond the creek he picked up the tracks again, so

plain a child would know at a glance that a horse had galloped along, just a few minutes ago. In the dust and gravel they were printed deep, here and there covered by Mike's tracks. If Farley were hidden somewhere watching, he would know what Chip was looking for; no doubt about it now. But that did not matter so much to Chip. He was after Wane's horse and saddle, and he meant to get them before he was through.

He retraced the tracks to the creek, crossed it slowly and came back. At the water's edge, where Farley had ridden in, the tracks ceased altogether.

14. A Killer Set Afoot

WHILE MIKE SIPPED WATER THROUGH HIS TEETH, CHIP warily eyed his surroundings. Down the creek was open land, reaching almost to the river. Above the crossing, however, the rock walls narrowed in until even now in slack water the creek flowed flush with the cliffs, the stream half choked with cobblestones and boulders. From where he was, the ravine looked long and unbroken with the side gullies. And yet, Cash Farley and his horse had not dissolved into thin air. Had he been in ambush somewhere, watching, he certainly was slow about shooting. With tight-lipped stubbornness, Chip reined Mike upstream, to the complete demoralization of a school of young trout.

For a dozen rods or more it was tricky going. The rock walls leaned inward, and boulders clogged the channel until he was almost tempted to turn back. Yet he kept on, giving Mike his head and encouraging him in low tones to keep at it. In high water it would be impossible to ride a horse up that creek. Even now there were pools where Mike waded carefully, the water over the stirrups at times. Chip began to feel dubious. Yet Farley must have come this way, since there was no other. Down the creek he would have been in plain sight. He had not gone on along the trail, else there must have been tracks to betray him. And certainly he had not turned back.

The creek gave an abrupt twist with the thrust of rock ledge out toward the opposite wall. Chip doggedly followed the turn and came out unexpectedly into a long flat valley, in some places nearly a quarter of a mile across. He was as surprised as a fly must feel after it has crawled down inside the neck of a beer bottle and suddenly discovers space all around it. On either hand the rocky walls receded, lumping themselves up into ridges, knolls and little pinnacles. And where the right wall shied away from him, a dim trail left the creek bed and ran on down the flat, weaving in and out among the stunted sage.

A strange place. High water must cover the flat completely. Other times it certainly was a treacherous bog of gumbo mud. It could not be the main route to Big Butch's camp, Chip saw at a glance. Yet it was used occasionally, as the tracks testified. Furthermore, away at the other end of the flat, a small dust cloud moved swiftly. Chip immediately set about making a cloud of his own, and seeing to it that his cloud moved faster than the one he was following.

Galloping steadily, Mike lessened the distance

between. They were out of that valley into another, however, before the horseman ahead became definitely visible as a black object leaping rhythmically along in the dust kicked up by his horse. Chip leaned forward, a quick movement instantly answered by his horse. "Get him, Mike!" he cried between closed teeth, and Mike laid his ears flatter to his head as his stride lengthened.

Soon, that pace told. The bobbing black object ahead of them took shape. The horse became recognizable as a sorrel; then he was unmistakably Wane's horse, Dude, gallantly giving the best he had in him to a brutal rider who always wanted more.

In a moment Farley's black-mustached face came into view as he turned an inquiring glance over his shoulder. Chip waved him down and shouted. "Hey! Wait a minute! Got something to tell yuh!" And, surprisingly, Big Butch's head killer jerked his horse to a walk as Chip came pounding up to him.

The very audacity of the thing made it possible. Cash Farley never dreamed a man would come at him like that save in friendship. Still, he might have shown an instinctive caution by drawing his gun—but Dude stubbed his toe at the exact psychological moment, and Farley's attention was averted for the seconds it took Chip to draw his gun.

"Get your hands up—high!"

Murder was in Cash Farley's eyes, but his hands rose obediently, even with his hat crown. As neatly as if he had rehearsed the scene, Chip pulled Farley's guns one at a time from their holsters and threw them as far as he could send them into a dry wash off to the side of the trail.

"What the hell?" snarled Farley, wincing as Chip's left hand prodded for the bulge of a shoulder holster.

"Pull it out and throw it where the other two went. And don't make any bobble, because I feel like killing you, anyway." Chip's gun reached over and thrust its muzzle hard against Farley's spine.

"Who the hell are you? Billy the Kid?" But Farley was extremely careful to handle the third gun with his finger tips and to send it whirling end over end after the others.

"I'm Wane Bennett's brother. Does that mean anything to you?"

"Not a gee-damned thing. Didn't know 'im."

"I think you're lying. This is Wane's horse you're riding. Pile off him—and be damned quick about it."

Cash Farley piled himself off and he did it quickly. Chip reached out with his free hand and caught a bridle rein, but he did not take his eyes off the blaspheming Farley.

"Cut that out. Where's the rest of Wane's stuff? Where's his other horse?"

"How the hell'd I know?" Farley backed off, eyeing Chip malevolently. "Why don't you ask Milt Cummings?"

"I'm going to. But I'm asking you now. Who's got Wane's other horse? A gray, branded EB. Better tell me, Farley."

"Butch might have the gray. I don't know." Farley licked his lips. "Not for sure. Might be in a bunch Butch picked up last spring. I dunno."

That seemed likely and Chip let it pass. "Who worked the brand on his horse? He was an EB. Who made it a Window Sash?"

"I dunno. Butch, maybe."

Chip's lip curled. "Seems to be a whole lot you don't know," he sneered. "What really did happen to my brother?"

Cash Farley looked up at him with swiftly dilating pupils—mark of the man whose secret is in danger, had Chip only known it. He looked at the gun remorselessly aimed at his middle, glanced again into the cold, implacable face which at that moment lost its youth. His eyes shifted toward the draw which held his guns.

"Well?" Chip prompted in a colorless tone that yet seemed relentless.

"Ask them that knows. I wasn't there."

"You heard what happened, though."

"I heard he drownded in the river."

"You know he didn't. Just what did happen? Hurry up!"

"I don't know. That's straight; I don't." Farley took a breath. "Cow Island's the place to find out—maybe." He spat out the last word as a cautious afterthought, then added a little to it for good measure. "I'm only guessin'."

"Yes—like hell you are." Chip looked sidewise at Dude, brought his stern gaze back to Farley. "I ought to shoot you for the way you've been abusing this horse. Walk on up the trail—and don't look back as long as you're within reach of a bullet, or you'll sure get one. *Vamos!*"

Calling Chip foul names under his breath, Cash Farley moved sullenly up the trail. For a good hundred yards Chip followed him, sitting on Dude's rein ends because he needed a hand free for his gun, which still looked bleakly at Farley's back. When he stopped finally, he still kept both horses sidling and trampling the loose soil, effectively erasing any possible boot tracks—just in case.

When Farley at last ventured a glance over his shoulder, he must have been surprised to see that he had not put half as much distance between himself and Chip as he thought he had. And it was probable that he would not suspect the ruse but would go from where Chip now waited, straight down into the dry wash, looking for his guns. At least, that was Chip's hope. And with a last warning gesture Chip turned back and trotted away, holstering his gun with the satisfied air of a man who had done exactly what he set out to do.

15. "They'll Come A-Shootin'"

WITH BUT A CURSORY GLANCE AT THE SIX PERSPIRING boys who were wabbling through a three-legged race, Weary Willie sidled through the yelling, hooting crowd until he got within nudging distance of Cal Emmett. "Say, Cal! Yuh seen anything of Chip, lately?"

"Chip? Nh-nh. Seen him with a bunch of girls, awhile back. Off sparkin' one of 'em, chances *is. Whee-ee!* Go to it, Freckles!" Cal turned his round blue eyes away from the race then, meaning to ask Weary what it was he wanted of Chip. But Weary was gone, so Cal devoted himself again to rooting valiantly for his favorites, two freckle-faced boys from the Hobble O.

Weary hunted through the crowd until he came upon a group of four: Slim, Shorty, Happy Jack and Ted Culver. He squeezed in behind them and shot his question over Slim's shoulder. "Any of you fellows seen Chip around here?"

Shorty turned half around and gave him a quick, searching glance. "No. Why? Anything wrong, Weary?"

Weary Willie gave his head a worried shake. "N-no, only I can't find hide nor hair of him. I' been back up in the grove—"

"He was up there with a bunch of girls," Ted Culver spoke up. "Candy kid, all right—the way they was flockin' around him. Why don't you ask Julie Lang or some of them Rocky Point fillies?"

"I did ask Julie. She don't know a thing about him since the picnic. Kinda lookin' for him herself, the way she talked."

"Well, by golly, way he was standin' in with the girls, you better go round a bunch of 'em up. If they ain't got 'im, it's a cinch they know where he is," Slim advised.

"Chances is, he's off tryin' to git another whack at Tom Shaner," Happy Jack suggested with his usual pessimism. "Don't go lookin' fer no girls. You find Shaner, and I betcher you'll find Chip, all right; er what's left of 'im, anyway."

"Oh, come off your perch!" Weary retorted witheringly. "There's Tom Shaner, standin' right over there. What's the matter with yuh?"

"Where's Milt Cummings?" Ted Culver asked shrewdly.

"Oh, I've got Milt located, all right. He's with Julie Lang, back on the porch. Got a grand-stand seat."

At that moment, as the crowd shifted after the race, Jack Bates and Penny came up.

"Oh, hello, you fellows. Where's the rest of the boys?" Penny inquired— somewhat exuberantly—he and Jack having just come out of the saloon.

"Cal's over there—or was. Say, you boys seen anything of Chip lately?"

No, they hadn't; not since the picnic. And they rather monotonously mentioned Chip's evident popularity with the girls.

Weary Willie shrugged his shoulders and walked away from them without replying to the implication that Chip was off philandering. He knew better. Chip wasn't that stripe, and it didn't matter how many girls had hung around him at the picnic. It sure wasn't Chip's doing.

He didn't know where else to look, unless it was down where the horses had been left. Though he would never confess it to a soul, he had already strolled up past that cellar of gruesome history, just to make sure that it was still empty and with the door open. He was passing the Lang porch when Julie Lang came down the steps and spoke to him. Weary halted in his tracks, a little startled if the truth were known. He had no wish to antagonize Milt Cummings if he could help it. He had always liked Milt. But Milt, he saw with a quick side glance, was no longer on the porch, nor anywhere in sight.

"I just wondered—have you found Chip Bennett yet?" Julie asked, in what she probably intended for a careless tone. "I'm afraid I offended him, up in the grove, and I just thought maybe I'd better explain— before he declares war."

Weary's grin answered her light tinkling laugh. "Well, he sure will have to do some explaining himself, quick as I get him located," he drawled. "I was just going down to see if he was keeping his horse company. Chip's funny that way. Gets spells of kinda ganging off by himself—don't want to talk to nobody. Then again he's full of the devil and joshin' anybody that comes along. I guess all this crowd—well, when you've lost all your folks, I imagine the more people's around you, the lonesomer you get. I know I was that way when I first run away from home. I'm getting kinda used to it now. Been away going on two years."

Julie had strolled off down the road with him, leaving the crowd yelling and clapping over some new comedy race. She looked mighty sweet, Weary thought, holding those blue ruffles up out of the dust with one hand, and pushing back curls which the hot breeze kept pulling from under her blue-flowered white hat, and holding onto that hat between times. Girls sure had a hard time of it, the kind of clothes they had to wear. Took both hands to hold themselves together, seemed like. Good thing they didn't have to get out and punch cows, the way they had to dress. Sure good to look at, though; all them little ruffles—Weary would bet there were all of a dozen little narrow rows of ruffling on that skirt of Julie's. One above the other, from the bottom one swishing just free of the ground, to the top one cinched in under that blue ribbon she wore tied at the side with long streamers hanging down. Weary sure wished he could have that ribbon to tie to his bridle and braid in his horse's mane. It sure would look swell. He was so preoccupied with his thoughts about her that he failed to hear much of what she was saying. Just polite talk, he gathered. Nothing he needed to answer except with his perennial wide grin.

"Oh, here's Hec," she announced suddenly, while Weary was still mooning along beside her. "We'll ask him, and maybe it will save you a trip clear down there. Oh, Hec!" she called, before Weary could speak. "Have you seen anything of young Chip Bennett? You know—Wane's brother?"

Whereupon Hec stopped, pried off a chew of tobacco from a fresh plug, and replied that he had seen young Bennett for the last time on earth, more'n likely. He was explaining in detail just why he thought so, when Weary stopped him.

"Wait. You folks go over there under that tree, outa the sun, and wait till I go get the boys," he commanded in a crisp tone wholly unlike his usual easy drawl. He went off, taking long strides that covered the ground almost as fast as a run, and in a surprisingly short time he was back again with the Happy Family hurrying along with him. They arrived at the tree in a close, intent group.

"Now, tell that again, Hec. You say Chip saw Cash Farley riding Wane Bennett's horse and saddle. How long ago was that?"

Hec squinted up at the sun, pulled out a tarnished goldine watch and snapped open the case for a comparison of the time. "Two hours ago; all uh that; mebby two hours and a half. He drug me down there t' where his horse was at, so'st he wouldn't waste no time gettin' all the low-down on Cash and them fellers. An' then he started off like the devil was after him."

"After Cash Farley?" gasped Julie. "Oh, the foolish, crazy boy! Why, he'll be *killed!*"

"Come on, boys. We better be hitting the high spots," Shorty interposed, and led the way out into the vivid sunshine. "Go on, Hec. What all did he say?"

Hec flung out a hand. "Oh-h—just asked where Big Butch's camp was—things like that. I *told* 'im he'd git killed sure. I sure talked m'self black in the face, boys, tryin' to keep 'im here. I told 'im to stay away from that bunch. And all he said was, 'Like heh—like fun I will!'" Hec quoted, with a hasty elision because of Julie's presence.

"And he started out?" Shorty's tone was grim.

"He shore did. And I was down talkin' to Turk, a while back. Turk says he crossed over on the ferry— same way Cash crossed—and he shore was loadin' up fer bear, on the way out. Filled his six-gun and his rifle both. Turk knowed it was the Bennett boy, on account of him lookin' so much like Wane."

"Get going, boys," Shorty ran the last few steps to his horse.

Cowboys are trained to speed in getting under way, but it is doubtful if Jim Whitmore's Happy Family ever made ready to leave camp in less time than they did it now. With the brim of her blue-flowered white hat nipped in between left thumb and forefinger, and with her blue ruffled dress held up at the side with her right hand, Julie watched them with wide, purple eyes. She said again, "Oh, the foolish, foolish boy!" But no one heard her; or if they did, they gave no heed.

Weary was first up. Reining his horse out into the open, he gave a yell. "Well, mamma mine! About time you was showing up!" He gave a shaken laugh. "We was just getting ready to start out and pick up the pieces!"

Trotting two tired horses into the group, Chip swung down unsmilingly, touching his hat to Julie Lang as he came to the ground. "Sorry you fellows got excited over my absence," he said coldly. "I had an errand and it couldn't wait." While they looked at one another foolishly, he pulled the saddle off Dude and with a twisted wisp of hay began rubbing him down. But after all he was only a boy. The sight of an angry red saddle sore on Dude's withers broke his stoical silence. His bleak eyes went from face to face in quick stabbing glances.

"I wish I'd shot him when I had the chance!" he gritted furiously. "Look at that back! Look at his flanks! You'd think he'd been ridden by a mountain lion, the way he's ripped with those spurs of Cash Farley's; rowels caked with blood and hair—and I let him live, the damned dirty skunk!"

135

"Well, you got the horse back," Shorty checked him with the quiet reminder. "If you took him out from under Cash Farley, like Hec, here, told us—boy, you sure are a wonder!"

"Yeah. How'd you cut the mustard, Chip?" Cal Emmett wanted to know. "Cash Farley's a killer, according to what folks say about him."

Chip looked across at him. "He sure as—anything wasn't working at it today," he snorted.

"Go on and swear if you want to," Julie Lang invited him unexpectedly, coming up closer. "I want to hear how you did it, Chip. Didn't you have a fight, or—or *anything?* I don't see how you'd *dare*—"

"Why, there wasn't anything to it," Chip said in an embarrassed tone, his eyes softening as they dwelt upon her. "I just took after him and kept fogging right along till I overhauled him. He was off on one of their secret trails by that time, away back in the hills. I guess he thought I was somebody he knew, or that was sent after him with a message or something. Because when I yelled at him to wait, he waited. So I just rode up close and pulled down on him with my gun. I told him to pile off and he did. That's all." It was not the heat alone that reddened his face when he finished.

"Ma-ma mine! And him a two-gun man!" breathed Weary.

"He wasn't any kind of a gun man when I got through pitching his guns into the gully." Chip's mouth twitched into a faint smile. "He had three on him when I started in. I don't know how many he found after I'd left him and come back."

"Well I'll be—switched!" Ted Culver exclaimed in an awed tone.

"Left 'im alive, yuh say?" Hec glanced sidelong at Julie, walked off a few steps and spat modestly into a bush.

"Why, certainly I left him alive." Chip frowned.

"Too bad!" drawled Hec, shaking his head. "You oughta killed 'im when yuh had the chancet. Now you'll have the hull kit an' caboodle out gunnin' for yuh."

"Oh! Do you think they will, Hec?" gasped Julie.

"Shore they will. If Chip here had put a bullet in Cash, Big Butch and his bunch wouldn't 'a' knowed who done it, chances is. Not unless they caught Chip ridin' that horse, or some'pm."

"That's right," Shorty soberly agreed. "You sure have stirred up a hornet's nest, Chip."

Of a sudden Chip exploded into swift speech. He picked up the saddle, swung it upon one bent knee and pointed a shaking finger while his eyes bored into their faces.

"All right, let them come. I'll meet the whole gang of them. You see this saddle? Wane planned that—had it made to order. See that stamped border? I drew that design to fit the saddle. Look here, all of you. I drew Wane's name in here—both sides the same. See that G? G-a-w-a-i-n. In my writing, copied into the pattern, because print letters would show. See this bridle? An old cowpuncher that used to work for my father made that head-stall for Wane's twenty-first birthday. And I earned the money to buy him those conchos to put on it, and that silver-mounted bit. See this horse? Wane broke him to ride—and he used this saddle and bridle to do it. My father gave him his pick out of the bunch on that same birthday, and he picked this sorrel. Dude—" He stopped, swallowed, bit his lip hard for control.

"And here today," he went on fiercely, "I saw him tied up there in front of the saloon—looking like a string of suckers. Look at him! Look at that sore back and those ribs! Do you suppose he was ever abused that way when Wane was alive?

"Of course I went after him!" he cried hotly. "I'd have got him if I had to fight Big Butch and all his gang. Fight—nothing!" The fury seeped out of his voice as he hunched his shoulders with contempt. "If Cash Farley's a sample of your killers—"

Hec Grimes craned his long thin neck toward the river. "You ain't through with this yit," he stated sententiously. "They'll be down on yuh like a thousand uh brick. Cash'll raise the gang and they'll be after yuh for that. You mark my words. Quick as he gits the word to 'em, what you done to 'im. Throwed his guns in a gully! My gosh, there ain't no livin' man ever done that before—not to Cash Farley, they ain't." He spat reflectively. "They'll come, and they'll come a-shootin'; you mark what I tell yuh."

"Oh, they will!" Julie Lang cried, almost in tears. "You don't know them!"

"Do you?" For the first time Chip spoke directly to her, and his eyes searched her face.

"I've—I've waited on them in the dining room, more

than once. In a hotel you can't pick and choose—"

"Well, I can," Chip said shortly. "I don't run a hotel."

"You can pick a fight, all right," Julie flashed back at him. "I never saw a fellow rush into trouble the way you do. Now you've got what you went after, the best thing you can do is ride straight for Flying U ranch. All of you. If you don't go right away, before Cash rounds up the rest of the gang, they'll ambush you sure as the world."

"You bet they will," Hec worriedly attested. "They ain't goin' t' let yuh git away with nothin' like that, boy. No, sir. When you set Cash Farley afoot an' throwed his guns inta that gully, you shore as h—the world stirred yourself a mess uh trouble. No two ways about that."

"All right, let it ride that way," Chip answered him shortly. "The rest of you fellows ain't concerned in this at all. It's my own personal affair."

"Oh, ain't we?" Weary made ironical reply to that. "Try and keep us out!"

"Oh, do go home—before they come here!" pleaded Julie, tears brimming her eyelids. "They'll see by your tracks that you came back here— You don't *know* Big Butch's gang! They'll stop at nothing, once they start."

"Same here." Chip gave her a diffident smile. "I'm sorry, but I can't go yet. I've got to see Milt Cummings."

"Milt? What's he got to do with—"

"You see," Chip told her gently, "I want to know how Cash Farley happened to get hold of this horse and saddle. And there's another horse and quite a lot of Wane's stuff I'd like to locate." Then he added a statement that made every man there draw in his breath. "I've got to know what really did happen to Wane. Cash Farley told me Cow Island's the place to find out."

16. A Boy in Love

"WELL," SAID JULIE, STEPPING DAINTILY AROUND A dead branch that had fallen into the path, "of course, if you want to go right ahead with no concern and no consideration for other people's feelings, I suppose there's nothing I can say to stop you."

Having signaled with her eyes for the others to go back by themselves and leave her to handle Chip, Julie was showing him a shady path homeward by way of the picnic grove, which was yet some distance ahead. Chip had hesitated, somewhat embarrassed at the openness of taking a walk with Julie Lang right then, when the whole bunch knew about it; but they had seemed to take it for granted he'd go when she asked him, if he didn't want to get in the shade and take a shortcut back; they had gone off without a look in his direction. And here he was, walking with his Goldilocks as he had dreamed of doing, and they were closer to quarreling than Chip would have believed possible; he was getting no satisfaction whatever out of the walk.

"Girls seem to have very peculiar ideas," he said coldly. "I don't see why you think Milt Cummings or any one else has a right to my brother's property. Milt probably owed him wages, at that. I'm not trying to collect anything. All I expect to do is get Wane's stuff together and take care of it. He'd want me to. If he knows, he must hate to see his horses abused and his things kicked around by men that aren't fit to lick his boots. And if he doesn't know—well, I do, and I won't stand for it a minute longer than is necessary." He turned a troubled, half-angry look down at her. "So what's so selfish and inconsiderate about that?"

Julie stooped to pick a cluster of "Indian paintbrush" glowing vividly beside a bush. With a pretty gesture of shy venturesomeness and a smile that promised all he dared to demand, she turned, bit off a stalk and pushed the red blossom in Chip's button-hole. With a provocative pat or two and her head tilted sidewise, she looked up into his face and smiled again breathtakingly. "Nothing selfish about that, silly," she said, in a soft caressing tone. "The selfishness would be in rushing up to Milt right now, when every one is having a good time, and demanding your brother's things. If he has them, of course they're all out to the ranch; the Lazy Ladder. It—it wouldn't make him feel any friendlier toward you, if you dragged him away from the dance—"

"I don't want him to feel friendly toward me." But Chip's eyes had begun to glow and his mouth had its youthful curve again. "I don't feel any too friendly toward him, if you want to know."

"Foolish, foolish," she said in that make-believe scolding way she had sometimes. "I do believe you're jealous."

"Yes-s?" Chip had discovered certain caressing tones in his own voice; tones that brought the color to Julie's cheeks.

141

"Well, you've no—cause to be." She had almost said, "no right to be," but she changed that just in time. "I've known Milt ever since I came into the country with Uncle Barr. Ages ago."

"Yes, I can see you're ancient," grinned Chip. But the other subject obtruded itself even into this fascinating little byplay. "Can't you see, Goldilocks, I've got to do—all I can? Wane hasn't got anybody else to—take his part and look after him; his stuff. And I've got a feeling he didn't just fall off his horse and drown, as some people try to make out. It's my business to find out what happened." A sudden thought sharpened his gaze. "Do you know, Goldilocks?"

She gasped, pulled free the hand he was holding. "I? Why, for heaven's sake! What makes you think—"

"You're where you hear things," he told her disarmingly. "Look how you knew about me, down in that cellar. I thought maybe you might know—"

"It was Hec told me about you," she said quickly. "I saw Tom and Dave Burch talking to you, and then Shaner led off your horses. So I asked Hec about it." She shivered a little and caught him by the arm, shaking it a little as she pulled him again into their leisurely stroll. "Of course I don't blame you a bit for the way you feel. I'd be the same, in your place. All I ask is for you to wait."

"I thought you wanted me to hurry up and get outa here," Chip said dryly. "I thought Big Butch was coming to massacre me."

"I was excited then. It—I was so scared at what you'd done, Chip; the horrible risk you took, going after Cash

Farley like that. They won't come. Not right today. There's too many people here that have got it in for them. No, they'll watch their chance and try and catch you when you aren't expecting them.

"No," she said with real earnestness, looking up into his face, "I just want you not to spoil all the fun. Tomorrow—any other time will do as well. Better. Why, think how all those Flying U boys must have planned and looked forward to this doings. If you start anything like that, they'll all buy in; you know they will. You heard what Uncle Barr said, about you all being a Happy Family and sticking together. They do, too. Look how they were all ready to start out and hunt you up—every single last one of them. They'd have tackled Big Butch and his whole gang, if anything had happened to you, Chip."

"Yes, I guess they would, all right."

"So the least you can do for them is to let them go ahead and enjoy themselves. Don't you see? Tomorrow, this will all be over and everybody gone home, and then you can speak to Milt about Wane's stuff. It will be all right then. Of course, he'll turn everything over to you. Why shouldn't he? Milt's all right, only you just don't like him. But that's no reason why you should spoil everybody's good time."

When she put it in that light, Chip saw himself as a bone-headed yahoo that didn't give a darn for anybody but himself. His face grew hot with shame.

"You *will* promise me you'll wait, won't you—dear?"

That last word, the tone in which it was spoken, thrilled him as once before it had done. With no real consciousness of what he was doing, he caught her close in his arms.

"I guess there isn't anything in the world I wouldn't promise you, Goldilocks," he said in a shaken, low voice, his face bent toward her. What else he said, he could not afterwards remember. He did not try. He was eighteen, and this was the most sublime, the most intoxicating moment of his whole life. He had never loved a girl before now. At that moment he believed implicitly that this was her first moment of love. Beneath his finger tips her heart was throbbing. . . . It reminded him of a broken-winged meadowlark which he had caught and held cupped in his hand one day as he was riding north. Its heart had beaten so fast with terror of him. . . . But Goldilocks wasn't afraid of him. Goldilocks was . . .

Suddenly he tilted her face up, stared deep into her eyes. "Do you love me?" he whispered with a terrible intentness, yet smiling too, because he thought he knew.

"Silly!" she whispered back, smiling up at him. "Isn't that a foolish question?"

He kissed her then, shyly, earnestly, as a boy would kiss when first he loved. And held her strongly, staring straight ahead, seeing nothing, unprepared for the over-whelming wish that his mother and Wane might know of this gift of God that had come to him so unexpect-edly. His mother would love his little Goldilocks. And Wane—Wane had loved her once . . .

The thought shook him out of his trance. He turned her face again to his, tilting it back, his fingers underneath her chin. "Did you love Wane?" he demanded with abruptness.

Julie gasped. He saw the widening of her eyes—the pupils little black pools rimmed with dark blue.

"Why—Chip! What a question!" Then, seeing the three lines come between his straight dark eyebrows, she lifted a hand and pulled his fingers away, freeing her chin. "You hurt," she said. And she added, "You're so strong!" And after that, since he still was silent, "I—*liked* Wane. He was a fine young man, Chip. You're a lot like him. Did any one ever tell you?"

"Yes."

Julie laughed her sweet, tinkling little laugh. "I expect Wane had plenty of sweethearts. All the girls were crazy about him. I always enjoyed talking with him," she added primly. "He was so—so different from most of the fellows—"

"Wane loved you, didn't he?"

Julie pulled herself from his embrace. She straightened her hat, tucked in a tightly crimped lock of hair. Then she pinched in a fold of blue ruffled skirt and lifted it stylishly at the side. "What a question!" she said reprovingly, as she started on along the path. "I told you we were friends." She smiled distractingly over her shoulder at him. "All the boys aren't as foolish—and as dear—as you are, Chip."

"He did love you. I know he did. He couldn't help it." Chip's eyes were rather tragic in their earnest seeking of the truth in her face.

"That's just your silly notion. Come on. We'll be talked about, if we don't hurry back. We'll go to the picnic grove where we can swing; maybe, if the kids aren't at it still."

"What about Milt Cummings? He's stuck on you—"

"I don't like that word," frowned Julie.

"But you like the man, don't you?"

"Why, of course. You're just about the only one who doesn't like him." Julie walked a little faster.

"How about that argument you had with him that time? Over that bargain he broke and wanted you to keep."

"Oh, that! Why, that was ages ago."

"Less than a month. How did you come out, Goldilocks?"

"Why, we—we compromised. Milt isn't as bad as you think." They were at the edge of the picnic grove, empty now save for clusters of squealing small children around the two swings. Julie hurried her steps. "Now be a good boy, Chip, and don't imagine you have to be jealous of every man in the country. That means you don't trust me. Look at those poor little tads trying to push those big heavy swings. Let's give them some fun, shall we?"

Chip did not object, though his enthusiasm was not marked by any hilarity. He had been lifted out and away from his brooding trouble into a world of warmth and happiness. He was not alone, he never would be alone again, because his Goldilocks loved him. Her rebuke of his jealous questioning shamed him, yet left him glad. This squealing, yelling crowd of small fry clamoring to be swung high and long served only to push his thoughts inward, where he could realize the full import of those few minutes back there on the shady path.

Even to Julie Lang, gracefully swinging the smallest tots in the low swing hung for their special convenience—even to Julie Chip's thoughts were unrevealed by look or word or manner. If she wondered at all about them, she must have decided that he was giving himself wholly to the work at hand. Certainly he was no bungler at it and he gave perfect satisfaction.

With the flat of his palms pressed firmly against gingham shirt and the muscular young shoulders of a boy beneath it, he sent the big swing far out and up into the branches of near-by trees. Methodically he counted to twenty-five, then caught the ropes as they came back and ejected that reluctant customer to let the next one wriggle into firm position on the seat, sitting squarely in the middle lest the swing go crooked. If a little girl was next, he did not push quite so hard, though the count was inexorably the same. No please and no excuses. Not letting the old cat die. Twenty-five was the turn. No more, no less. Then make way for the next.

But all the while he was seeing the shadows fall softly across the trampled brown loam, the dried leaves of summer gone by. He was seeing the high flitting from tree to tree as worried birds sought their accustomed roosting places but feared to remain because of the clamor below. Though he dared not look that way often, he was seeing Goldilocks softly swaying in the low swing not too near for safety; Goldilocks with her hat off and her hair like dull gold in the shadow; Goldilocks with her blue ruffled skirt trailing on the leaf mold, swaying there with one round young arm reaching up to grip the ropes, a small child on her lap and a solemn-eyed little boy hanging on tightly by her side.

He was seeing her as his girl, all others as pale images walking through the years, all men keeping their distance because she belonged to him, now and forever more. He was counting the years until he would be twenty-one and could take up land, build a home for Goldilocks. Three years; two-and-a-half years, to be exact. Well, there was no law against his working and saving and getting a little bunch of cattle together. Jim Whitmore would let him run them in his herd. He thought gloatingly of his horses. Silvia would have another colt next spring. Since Wane was gone, Silvia was his; Rummy too. He'd break Rummy to ride, in another couple of years. Have him gentle as a kitten, ready for Goldilocks when they set up housekeeping on that ranch he'd take up.

A boy's dream, but he believed it so invincibly that Milt Cummings, walking up through the grove, could not shake his faith in it. Milt Cummings would get a pretty stiff jolt, one of these days. He certainly would, if he had his sights raised to marrying Miss Julie Lang!

"Oh, hello, Milt! Want to have a swing?" Julie skidded the small child off her lap as she rose, laughing. The solemn little boy wabbled and slid down by himself. "We've been holding the calf herd. What have you been doing?"

"Drifting around." Milt slanted a look at Chip, who was swinging a little girl and impassively counting aloud, "—twenty! Twenty-one—twenty-two—"

"Oh, Chip! Have you been introduced to Mr. Cummings? Milt, this is Wane Bennett's young brother Chip." Julie's tone set back Chip's age to about fifteen, but Chip never noticed.

"—Twenty-three-ee—How da do, Mr. Cummings—twenty-five; and out you come."

"Howdy," Milt said, with as casual a manner as Chip had shown. "Dance is about to begin, Julie. We're supposed to lead the grand march together. Come on."

"Just a minute, Milt, till I gather up these young ones and shoo them down to their mothers. They'd stay up here till dark, I do believe. Are you coming now, Chip?"

"No, thanks. I don't feel like dancing. Hop in, sorreltop. It's your turn next. Sit in the middle. No, get over to the side and let this brockle-face feller in alongside. Have to double up on you now. It's getting around quitting time. All set? Back you come—let's *go!* One—two-o—"

But he saw Milt's arm slip around the blue figure moving out of sight down the slope. For one swing he forgot to count. Then his face cleared. Milt Cummings was just an old friend of hers. Sweet on her—trying to get a stand-in—but he sure had a jolt coming to him when he found out who it was Goldilocks really loved.

He wished she wouldn't let Milt take liberties like that—but he guessed she knew what she was doing. Afraid to make Milt mad, probably. Wanted to keep him in a good humor till Chip had his session with Milt. It was all right. Hell! Who'd want a girl he couldn't trust out of his sight?

17. The Happy Family Rides Herd

WITH THE COMING OF DUSK THE CROWD BEGAN TO change. Small ranchers with large families herded their progeny down to the camp ground, hitched up their teams, boosted their wives up over the front wheel to the seat, handed up the smallest children and saw to it that the others had settled to decorous behavior in the hay left in the wagon bed. Horsemen arrived, for the most part riding on to the saloon and new dance hall. Picnics had not appealed to these revelers. They had waited until the entertainment grew more to their liking; and these had a drink—or two or five—and hastened into the hall whence came the brassy blare of at least part of the army band from the fort, softened a little by the swish of starched petticoats and the shush-shush-shush of dancing feet slipping over the new floor.

In all this Chip had no part. For a time he stood just inside the doorway watching the dancers—watching Julie, as much as he dared. Weary came up and begged him to dance, then went back to his fun. Tom Shaner brushed in past him, suddenly recognized him and turned halfway around to glare. Milt Cummings honored him with quick measuring glances when he waltzed by with Julie in his arms; which he did as often as he could, in Chip's opinion. Now and then some one of his own outfit paused for a word or two, plainly wanting to help him feel at home but not knowing just how to go about it.

Then Cal Emmett, having do-si-doed, gents you

know, swung on the corner and swung his own, spied Weary edging down the hall between the dancers and the left-overs sitting stiffly on the benches ranged along the wall. Cal stepped back, mopping his face and neck with a blue silk handkerchief, and intercepted Weary.

"Better take a look around and see where Chip's went to," he muttered. "I seen him go outside, a while back—"

"*Third* couple out t' the right, do-si-do—" bellowed the caller just then, and Cal, being half of the third couple, caught his partner by the hand and went to do-si-do as he was commanded. But his round blue eyes turned for a last look at Weary while he was doing it, and the slight jerk of his head toward the door emphasized the urgency of Weary's duty. Needlessly, for Weary was already sufficiently concerned.

His alarm seemed a waste of energy, however. He had glanced into the saloon and had turned away when he saw Chip just going down the store steps next door, his coat pockets bulging and a package in his hand. In three long strides Weary overtook him. "What yuh got there?" he inquired amiably, bringing down his hand in friendly fashion on Chip's shoulder. "Firecrackers?"

"Gall cure." Chip pulled off the paper bag and showed him the tin box. "Ought to have fixed Dude's back before now."

"Mamma! Going off to doctor your horse when there's a corral full of pippins back there just dyin' to dance!"

"Well," drawled Chip, "they've got my permission. I'm not stopping them, am I?"

"You sure as hell ain't helping 'em any," Weary retorted. "Don't be a chump. Come on back and I'll make you acquainted with the swellest lookers in seventeen counties."

"Nothing doing," Chip told him gruffly. "I wouldn't dance if you was to trot out Lily Langtry herself."

"What's the matter? You and Julie have a run-in?"

"Not so you could notice," Chip denied emphatically before he realized what meaning Weary might attach to the words.

"Oh! 'I see,' says the blind man. I wondered why the sudden interest in your welfare—"

"Cut it out, Weary."

"All right, if you'll pull up your jaw and come on back there and dance. No use moping around like this, Chip, and you know it. Come out of it, why don't you? You ain't helping your brother any by acting this way."

They had stopped in the shadow of the house to talk. Two riders went past within ten feet of them, the nearest swinging his head automatically to peer at them as he went by, a huge figure in the saddle; not fat, not even of great bulk; but tall and with wide shoulders and a look of strength beyond the strength of ordinary men.

Chip gave them only a cursory glance, but Weary took a long breath and exhaled it in a sigh as the men rode on. "Ma-ma mine!" he whispered, pulling Chip back into deeper shade where they could still observe what went on in the street.

"What's eating yuh?" Chip grumbled restively.

"Big Butch and Cash Farley!" He craned down the road. "I wonder where's the rest of the gang? S'pose they're goin' to clean out the place, Chip?"

"You can search me," Chip offered with some impatience. "Let me go on and tend to my horse. I'm not afraid of 'em."

"No, 'cause you ain't got sense enough to be afraid. Butch is goin' into the store. Cash is on his horse, holding Butch's horse."

"Anything funny about that?"

"N-no—only in their bein' here atall."

"I s'pose even Big Butch might run out of matches now and then," Chip observed sarcastically. "Or even tobacco. We might go back and ask."

"Not on your life!" Weary's tone was low but fervent. "You stay right where you're at till we see what's on their minds."

Apparently nothing much was on the minds of Farley and Big Butch. In less than five minutes Butch came out, tied a bundle behind his cantle. Whether Chip and Weary noticed it or not, the area around dance hall and saloon was surprisingly empty of men. Not a person was in sight when Big Butch, having disposed his purchases to his liking, mounted and reined away from the store. Without a word, with no man seeking to stop them, they rode back down the road at a trot.

"Gosh!" Weary Willie exclaimed under his breath, when the two were gone. "One minute later comin' outa that store, Chip, and you'd of walked right into a flock of bullets from Cash Farley's gun!" And he added, to clinch the matter, "Just as sure as God made little apples, he never would pass up a chance like that."

"If he came with the idea of taking Dude away from

me—" hazarded Chip, and walked as fast as his long legs would let him.

"Ah, they weren't after that horse," Weary protested; but his long stride nevertheless kept pace with Chip's.

They need not have worried over that possibility, however. Dude was standing hipshot and half asleep over the remains of his hay pile. Sturdy Mike, beside him, was still munching. Other Flying U horses near by were standing bored but patient, where they had been tied. Off a little way toward the river a lighted lantern moved slowly, weaving in and out among the thinned assemblage of teams and vehicles.

"They'd have to hunt around some to find Dude over here," Weary remarked. "In and right out again—I wish I knew what the devil those two were after."

"I thought I said matches," drawled Chip, more indifferently than he felt. Though he never would admit it, an odd prickling of his scalp had not yet subsided. That one minute of grace which Weary had mentioned was about the closest he had ever been to death, he told himself with an inward shiver. Weary was absolutely right, he knew. Cash Farley never would have let a chance like that slip by. Back there on the trail he had sworn that he would kill Chip—he had named several horrible ways of doing so.

Footsteps came hurrying. "That you, Weary? Where's Chip at?" Cal Emmett's voice called guardedly. And when Chip answered that he was there, Cal swore with relief. He said the rest of the boys were on their way, wanting to know if Chip were all right. The word was being passed around up there at the dance that Big

Butch and Cash Farley were in town. And if that was the case, they'd better get their artillery ready.

The lantern came weaving their way, borne by the ubiquitous Hec Grimes. They fairly pounced upon him. But Hec could offer little they did not already know. "You can search me, boys," he said uneasily. "I never was so took back in my life as I was to see them two ridin' past. I been down around here, kinda lookin' after things, like Barr told me t' do, an' I been kinda wonderin' if they'd dast to come across the river with the hull country here. 'Course, I was a little afraid the hull gang'd come over an' start a fuss; be just like 'em to. But them two alone, ridin' in an' right on out agin—"

"Which way, Hec?" Shorty's voice asked.

"Back acrost the river, the way they come. Took the ferry—like they always do. I guess they figure that if they're on that, they got a better chance of standin' off anybody that takes a notion to start something."

"I don't see how you figure that," Jack Bates argued. "I'd hate to be perched up on that scow in a fight. There ain't so much of a mark to shoot at in the water. Part of yuh's covered up."

"Yeah, but the way that ferry bobs along, it'd be awful easy to miss a feller, 'specially if you're wadin' acrost. And it's damn easy to git hit in the water, an' don't yuh ferget it. Can't handle yourself s'good. Git a bullet in yuh, and chances is you go on down the river same as—" With a startled glance toward Chip, Hec turned away, spat out his tobacco quid and forgot to finish what he had been saying. "Anyway," he added weakly, "they went on acrost the river. Peaceable."

"Down the river same as who?" Chip asked harshly, pushing toward Hec with the salve box still unopened in his hand. "You mean my brother, don't you?"

"Well, now," Hec evaded him, pausing to inspect his tobacco plug, "I was just surmisin' how a feller could git in a jackpot. I never—"

"Who shot my brother off his horse while he was in the river?" Chip persisted. "Cash Farley said I could find out right here at Cow Island, and if anybody knows, you do. Who did it?"

In the dim light of the stars, the lantern in Hec's hand and the moon that was brightening the east but had not risen yet, Hec eyed the other speculatively while he worried a corner off the plug. "You can search me—if anybody done it," he said at last. "You don't want to go around believin' anything Cash Farley says."

"You're just trying to cover things up, like everybody else," Chip cried bitterly. "I'm getting pretty damned tired of it, I tell yuh those. Somebody spread the word around that my brother was drunk and fell off his horse. And that's a damn' lie, and I know it. Wane wasn't a hard drinker. Then Shaner had to go and shoot off his mouth about how they hung Wane for a horse thief, and that's another damned lie. Now you come within an ace of letting the cat out of the bag and saying he was shot when he was crossing the river. That sounds the most plausible of anything I've heard yet. That's probably about what happened. Now, I want to know who did it!"

"Aw, I never said nobody did!" Hec protested, backing away from him. "What you wanta go off half-cocked like that for? All I said was—"

156

"I know what you said," Chip hotly broke in upon him. "You said plenty. Enough to go on, anyway. I'm getting damned sick of all this mystery, I'll tell you that much. Here I find one of your bad men riding Wane's horse, big as life—"

"He ain't my bad man," Hec nervously corrected him. "I don't have no truck with 'em."

"And the brand changed to the Window Sash. Who the hell owns the Window Sash, anyway?"

"Nobody, 't I know of." Hec rolled his eyes around the group, looking for support.

Men were edging up from among the scattered rigs. Probably from a distance the voices sounded as though a fight was brewing. Shorty stepped over and clamped his hand down on Chip's shoulder, and although he spoke quietly, his voice had in it a note of authority. "Go ahead and doctor your horse if you want to, while we water ours. This is no time or place to start digging into the past—there's other days coming, Chip; and if there ain't, it won't matter, anyhow. You take a fool's advice and let things ride the way they are for tonight."

"That's all right from your standpoint—Wane wasn't your brother," Chip said bitterly.

"If he was, I'd try and go at it calm. I wouldn't pick a Fourth of July dance—"

Chip twitched his shoulder loose and drew away toward Dude. "All right. Go on back and dance if you feel that way. I'll try and not upset your plans," he yielded gruffly.

Shorty looked at him a minute, then made an unobtrusive sign to the others. They began untying their horses, saying nothing at all to Chip. On their way to the river and back, they must have discussed his affair rather thoroughly, however, they were so studiedly cheerful on their return. They gathered what hay they could find to feed their horses, wrangled amiably among themselves and went off to the dance again, as if nothing in the world had happened or could happen to interfere with their pleasure.

They seemed not to notice particularly that Weary stayed behind with Chip, whose horses were not thirsty, and they gave no sign whatever of having conferred privately with Hec Grimes, who was to let them know at once if Chip rode off anywhere, or if any of Big Butch's crowd crossed the river.

They later treated Weary and Chip's arrival at the dance hall with as little apparent concern as if the two had merely walked into the mess house at home, when supper was ready. They neither urged Chip to dance nor paid him any particular attention for the rest of the night. Yet a keen observer might have noticed that not all of Jim Whitmore's Happy Family danced the same dance; and he might have wondered why it was that at least two of them lingered near the door—outside in the clear moonlight, preferably—smoking and loafing until they were replaced by others. Certainly Chip did not notice that the Happy Family "rode herd" that night. There were eight of them milling around in the crowd. Not once did it strike him as odd that some of the bunch should be within sight all the while.

But the Happy Family knew exactly how it had happened. Even when there was a fight in the saloon next door and everybody rushed to the spot, four Flying U cowboys stood outside with Chip, content to look through the window because he was not sufficiently interested to crowd inside.

They started home just when the moonlight was giving way before the dawn. Forty miles, and twenty-six uproarious hours without sleep, with a good deal of worry eating up their energy at the last. Slack in their saddles, they loafed along the trail, aching for their beds, wanting hot coffee and their bellies full of Patsy's grub. Even Chip, leading Dude with Wane's empty saddle mutely reminding him of the dead, seemed content to ride home without having faced Milt Cummings with the questions he meant to ask. Shorty was right, he thought drowsily. Better to make a special trip to the Lazy Ladder. He needed a long talk with Goldilocks, anyway. He wanted an understanding right away as soon as possible; not that they didn't already understand each other—but he supposed he ought to ask her straight out in so many words if she would marry him in about three years. Then they could begin to plan. And Milt Cummings would have to keep his distance. Julie wouldn't have to stand for Milt putting his arm around her—not when she was engaged to some one else.

He was dreamily deciding that he ought to send down to Denver to a store he knew and get a ring for Goldilocks. A plain gold ring, maybe, with their names inside; only he'd sure have them put Goldilocks on, instead of Julie. Maybe she'd want Chip instead of Claude. He guessed he'd better wait and ask her about that . . .

Just then, when they were no more than five or six miles from Flying U coulee, a familiar sound brought Chip's sleep-bowed head up with a jerk. Out of a rocky gully less than a hundred yards from the trail little Silver came hobbling painfully toward them, his left front foot held so that his hoof barely touched the ground when he walked. More than that, blood was caked brown upon his left shoulder, running down from a point at the roots of the last little tuft of his bushy red mane.

18. The Raid

"SILVER! WHAT THE DEVIL ARE YOU DOING OUT HERE?" Dismayed astonishment sharpened Chip's voice as he sent his horse lunging over to where the colt stood, shaking with fatigue and bewilderment.

With one accord the Happy Family charged after him, their own weariness forgotten in the plight of the colt. Springing from their saddles they surrounded him, for once almost speechless with amazement.

Shorty it was who bent his head beside Chip's, examining the wound. Abruptly he straightened, his face grim.

"Somebody shot him," he stated flatly. "That's a bullet hole there in his mane."

"Cash Farley," Chip declared in a choked tone. "That's why he never made a move to find me at Lang's." He stroked the colt's back and shoulder gently, his hand trembling. "Took it out on my horses, the damned dirty coward. I suppose we'll find Silvia and

160

Rummy around here somewhere—dead." His voice was dull and hopeless. His face had a ghastly, pinched look.

"Nope, you're wrong there, Chip," Shorty dissented hurriedly. "They run 'em off, most likely, and took a shot at the colt when he went lame. Here. Let's have a look at him."

Little Silver was a gentle thing. He stood with drooping head while Shorty lifted the lame leg and bent it across his knee. "Hunh! Got a knife, somebody? Rock stuck in his frog. He'll be all right, soon as I pry it out."

Half a dozen jack-knives were proffered eagerly as the boys crowded in a close huddle to watch. After a minute or two of expert gouging, a sharp-pointed triangular rock the size of a walnut dropped out into Shorty's palm. Breaths sucked in. Shorty turned it over, looked at it, was on the point of tossing it aside, when Chip reached out and took it from his fingers. "I'd like to sink that in Cash Farley's gizzard!" he said, with a bitterly youthful vindictiveness. "I will too, when I get my hands on him again."

"You oughta be damn thankful for that rock," Shorty observed sharply, letting the colt's foot down and straightening up to look at Chip. "If he hadn't of picked up that rock and went lame so he couldn't keep up, he'd be to hell an' gone with the rest of the bunch."

Some one behind him swore a violent oath as Shorty's meaning sank in. Chip looked up quickly from the rock in his hand. "You think they ran off all the horses?"

"I sure do. No use wastin' time lookin' around here, boys—the trail's hours old right now. You can see for yourselves, that bullet hole quit bleeding quite a while ago and the blood's dried hard. Better put a rope on him, Chip, and lead him in to the ranch. Weary, you can lead the sorrel. The colt ain't hurt much, kid. Don't you worry about him. Bullet went too high to do any damage much. Whoever done it was a damn poor shot, or else he was in a hurry and the light was poor." He sent a speculative glance around the gully mouth, nodded in agreement with his theory.

"Happened about the time we left Cow Island, probably. The moon was goin' down and the sun wasn't up yet, and this gully opens kinda towards the south. The colt was hobblin' along in a poor light for shootin'. Well," he added cheerfully, "that goes to prove they was in an almighty hurry, and mad enough at Chip to try an' kill the colt, instead of leavin' him for us to find and take back."

"Cash Farley," Chip said again between his teeth.

"Yeah—some of that bunch, anyway." And Shorty swore. "We was all so damn crazy to hell around at that dance—if we'd come on home about our business, we'd of caught 'em right in the act!"

"I betcha they got away with every horse on the ranch." Happy Jack offered gloomily. "I knowed they was up t' somethin' when they left Cow Island all s' fast."

"Well, come on! We ain't doin' any good here," cried Shorty, and flung himself into the saddle. They were off in a drumming flurry of dust, leaving Chip and Weary

162

to follow as best they could with little Silver.

They arrived to find things about as bad as they needed to be. Every horse on the ranch—and that was close to a hundred head, counting broomtails and half-broken broncs in the pasture—had been taken. J.G. had a bullet in his leg which Shorty, with a sharp knife blade seared in a candle flame, was already trying to dig out. A puckered streak along the side of his neck told how close another bullet had come. As Chip and Weary finished unsaddling and started for the mess house, Cal and Penny walked beside them and told the story of the raid.

"J.G. says he heard 'em ride past," Cal related. "Sleepin' in the tent, he heard the horses walkin', and the saddle sounds, and he thought it was us fellows comin' back."

"Lord, I sure wish it had of been!" Penny cut in distractedly.

"Who don't?" snapped Cal, and went on with his story. "So J.G. says he never thought no more about it, just turned over and was dozin' off again, but kinda listenin' too, for us to put up our horses and come on up and hit the hay."

"It was along about three o'clock in the morning," Penny explained.

"Yeah. Well, the next he heard was the bunch comin' on down from the pasture. He knowed damn well then that it wasn't us, so he jumps up and grabs his gun and slips on his boots and goes out in his shirt tail. And sure enough, there they was, hazin' the horses down past camp and not givin' such a hell of a damn whether anybody heard 'em or not. So he runs out and cuts loose at 'em as he goes."

"My God, if we'd only been here!" Weary lamented.

"Same here. The gall of 'em, ridin' right down past camp like that! Well, he says he started runnin' and shootin'——"

"Nothing the matter with *his* nerve!"

"I'll say there ain't. Anyway, the light wasn't any too good for gun work, but he thought he saw one feller he took to be Big Butch kinda weave around in the saddle. He ain't sure, because they was bouncin' bullets around him about that time, and one got him in the leg. And he says it felt like a bee or somethin' swiped him on the neck. He wilted down on the ground, but he never stopped shootin' as long as he had a bullet in his gun."

"And what does old Patsy do but come out and blaze away with that old Zulu shotgun of his'n!" Penny elaborated. " 'Course, he was too far off to hit anything. They was gone by that time. So there wasn't no more to be done about it."

"Nothin' but tie a rag around J.G.'s leg and wait for us to get back."

"And us loafin' along like we had all the time in the world!" sighed Weary. "Mamma! We'd oughta be shot for ever leavin' in the first place."

"I'm the one that's responsible for the whole thing," Chip said heavily. "Cash Farley egged 'em on, just to take a crack at me."

"Aw, that ain't it at all," Weary was quick to comfort him. "That bunch is professional horse thieves. Everybody in the country is wise to that. They know the

Flying U outfit rides about the best horses in the country, and I'll bet they've been layin' low, watching their chance to annex a bunch of 'em. They'd have done it, Chip, if you never had come into the country at all; and don't you forget it."

"Yes? That'll do to say. You'll never make me believe this wasn't Cash Farley's scheme to get my horses. I know. I'm the one that set him afoot and made a monkey of him yesterday. I heard him make his brags of what he was going to do to get even. This thing lays between him and me."

"Aw, come off!" jibed Cal. "It lays between Big Butch and the Flyin' U, and we're the lads that'll settle it. You lost three horses, and the outfit's lost around a hundred. Where'd you get off at?"

"That's all right," said Chip shortly, in the tone that gave the lie to his words. "Let it go that way, if you want to."

They found Jim Whitmore pale and sweating with the pain of Shorty's rough surgery; but he held the lump of lead in his fingers, eyeing it with as much interest as a small boy examines his first pulled tooth. The cabin reeked with carbolic acid, and just outside the door Shorty was emptying a basin of pinkish soapsuds and looking pretty sick.

But, bandaged and helpless though he was, J.G. on his bed was laying down the law with his accustomed vigor. "No sense in the hull bunch of yuh tearin' right out after 'em on played-out horses," he was grumbling, as Chip and Weary went in. "Some of you boys have got to stay here and keep things going. There's still some line ridin' to do on them cattle. And there's got to be a bunch of horses rounded up and brought in and whipped into shape. Can't count on gittin' back them horses they run off last night—and we've got to have a remuda ready for fall round-up."

Rising fever from his wound was making him more talkative than usual, but no one noticed it. He was speaking what was running through their own minds. He grimaced as he moved his bandaged leg to a new position, and spoke again, giving orders. "Shorty and Slim and Jack and Ted'll take the trail. Not now—you all of you look like you'd been drug through a knot hole backwards. Git some grub into yuh and then go and bed down somewheres and git some sleep, all of you. Nothin' gained by goin' off half cocked, and your horses need to rest up."

"They'll have a hell of a start on us if we lay around here all day," Ted Culver complained restively.

His boss gave a snort of impatience with such reasoning. "They'll hold them horses somewheres in the Badlands today, and try and shove 'em across the river some time in the night. After midnight most likely. That's where you'll head for. Get hold of Dave Burch and tell him what happened. He's been waitin' to git the evidence on Big Butch; now's the time to catch him red-handed, tell him. He's always got two, three men hangin' around his shop fer just such cases as this. You git Dave Burch on the job."

His eyes traveled round the room. "You four'll have till midnight to git back down to Cow Island crossing. Go along now—bed down in a cool place and git some rest. You don't have to start much before sundown."

Chip took a step toward the bed. "Mr. Whitmore, I want to get after those horses. This is all on my account it happened, anyway, and I feel I'm responsible. And they've got Silvia and Rummy and Jeff. And they shot little Silver. I've got a lot to settle with that bunch—"

Jim Whitmore eyed him glumly. "And you'd like nothin' better than to tie into Big Butch single-handed," he growled. "That ain't nerve, that's damn foolishness." He eased his wounded leg into another position, swearing under his breath at the pain. "You go on and git some sleep," he growled. "You've raised about hell enough for a kid your age." And he added, "Damn this leg, anyhow!"

"It isn't the age that counts altogether," Chip muttered rebelliously. But he went out with the rest of them, dragged a blanket and the tarp off his bed in the bunk house, snubbed Weary, who showed a disposition to go with him, and disappeared among the willows along the creek bank.

Presently he was back, however, and ate in scowling silence with the rest of the boys. Later they saw him going to the corral with a pan of warm water into which he had emptied a can of condensed milk. Going to feed the colt. Well, that was all right. He'd fuss around with Silver, doctor Dude's sore back again, visit with them awhile and curl up somewhere for a sleep. Too darn bad J.G. wouldn't let him go along, but they could see where he was right about it. Chip took altogether too many chances.

The day drowsed along toward late afternoon. In

J.G.'s cabin Patsy sat and smoked his vile black pipe and conned a Doctor Pierce's Almanac, moving his lips as he spelled out the long words. Between times he drove the flies off J.G.'s face when he dozed, or gave him a drink of water fresh from the spring. In the bunk house—down by the creek under the cottonwoods—wherever there were shade and a hint of breeze, some cowboy lay drugged with sleep, drawing more energy into his body for the strenuous times that were to come.

With the lengthening of the shadows around them they awoke, sat up, yawned and rolled cigarettes, remembered what lay before them and bestirred themselves. One by one they straggled in, wanting to know how J.G. was feeling before they went off to feed and curry their horses for the work ahead. But one was missing when they foregathered in the mess house for an early supper, and when Weary went to call him he returned with a worried look in his eyes. "Chip's gone," he said in the tone of disaster. "I've got a note here—it was tied on his saddle."

"On his saddle—hell!" swore Shorty. "I seen his saddle hangin' where he always keeps it, so I never paid any more attention. I thought he was maybe watering his horses down at the creek."

Whereupon it appeared that each man there had taken the same thing for granted. They had seen the saddle in its accustomed place and had taken it for granted that Chip was somewhere around. They had plenty on their minds, they declared, without riding herd on each other.

"Well, I sure thought about him," Weary confessed. "But I've found out it ain't healthy to crowd in on him when he gets these offish spells, so I've been leaving him alone till he came out of it. He always does, give him a little time.

"That saddle of his fooled me too. Then I just happened to notice his rope was gone and this paper was tied where the rope belongs." He held up a small piece of paper folded with the neat accuracy which marked everything Chip did. "It's for J.G." He hesitated. "Think I oughta give it to him now, or wait till mornin', when he'll maybe be feelin' better?"

"How the hell do we know, till we hear what's in it?" Shorty made impatient answer. "Read it out, why don't yuh? I guess it's nothing secret."

The note sounded like Chip Bennett. So much so that the boys could imagine they heard Chip himself speak the words:

"Mr. Whitmore, I have quit my job to go after my horses. I feel responsible for your horses being stolen and will try and get them back.
Yours truly, Chip Bennett
"P.S. Please see that Silver my colt is fed and taken care of and take it out of my wages till I get back."

"Well, the darned, nervy chump! The son-of-a-gun!" Shorty exclaimed in a flattened voice, while the Happy Family looked at one another blankly. "Come on, boys. We better get a wiggle on if we're going to head that kid off." On his way to the door he looked at Weary, who was still staring at the lines.

"Now, don't *you* go and fly the track, Weary. It's

169

likely he ain't got much the start of us and we'll over-
haul him. He's headed for the river—pulled out in the
lead because he knowed damn well I'd turn him back if
I caught him gettin' ready to start. The Old Man's
asleep, or was. Hold that back till he misses Chip. It's
likely I'll send him back with a bug in his ear before
J.G. even knows he went."

19. Chip Takes the Trail

CHIP WAS NOT HEADED FOR THE RIVER, AND HE HAD
more of a start than any of the boys would have
believed. And while he had not advertised his departure,
he had not been especially sly about it. He had per-
suaded little Silver to drink warm milk out of a tin pan
and had given the bullet wound in his neck careful
attention, and with an old handkerchief and creek water
he had washed off the dried blood and wiped the
shoulder carefully so the flies would leave the place
alone. He had also washed and salved Dude's sore back,
relieved to see that it was already showing improve-
ment. A little care in arranging the saddle blanket, and
Dude could be ridden while the galled spot healed.

It was when he went to return the pan to the mess
house that Chip's thoughts crystallized into a definite
purpose. Patsy was in J.G.'s cabin, the boys were all
asleep somewhere—not a soul in sight anywhere, not
an officious tongue to wag with argument or protest. He
could do as he thought best.

He thought it best to get a few things out of the bunk
house, which also happened to be empty. He got

170

another box of rifle cartridges, all the shells he could find for his six-shooter, some clean socks and an extra shirt. His slicker was rolled on his saddle and he had a blanket and tarp down by the creek. He rummaged quietly in his camp outfit, got an old-fashioned powder flask that held salt; his drinking cup, water-tight match box—not much, but enough for his actual needs.

From Patsy's supplies he took a few pounds of corn meal, a little coffee, all the sour-dough biscuits he could find and a generous lump of pot-roasted beef. With a couple of pounds of bacon, he had a small pack that would see him through several days. Then he went back to the bunk house and got his frying pan and a small blackened bucket with a lid. Bacon he could broil on the end of a stick held over coals. Corn-meal mush or pones and coffee required some sort of utensil.

Still the pack was small, easily carried on his saddle. The blanket and tarp he strapped on Dude's back, careful that it should not rub the sore. He took Wane's saddle. Why, he did not attempt to explain to himself, except that it was a better saddle than his own and he preferred to have it in his possession. At the last, however, he remembered to take his own rope and a couple of piggin strings he found handy. And he wrote the note to Jim Whitmore. In his present mood he felt absolutely justified in what he was doing. Having been ordered to stay on the ranch, he saw no way out save the one he took. While he was on the pay roll he had to obey orders—but there was no law against his quitting.

A free man, he could think as he pleased, do as he pleased, follow the line of reasoning which to him seemed most logical. It was not the reasoning of J.G. Whitmore; it was the reasoning of Chip Bennett. He had faith in it; enough faith to follow it, at any rate.

He was not "going off half cocked," as J.G. put it. He rather prided himself on his cool deliberation, his following plain common sense. It might be all right, he told himself, for a man with four or five hundred horses to head for the river and wait for a stolen hundred to cross. It didn't mean as much to Jim Whitmore to lose a hundred horses as it did to Chip Bennett to lose Silvia and Rummy and Jeff. He found it best not to dwell upon the thought of Silvia and Rummy in the hands of Cash Farley—a man who rode with blood and hair on his spur rowels. He was not the kid folks tried to make out, but the thought of Cash Farley having those two horses to abuse made him hot all over. He had to grit his teeth to keep from bawling like a baby. Thank God, he thought, they didn't have little Silver in their clutches.

So he was following his own ideas. In Colorado he had heard the miners talk. There was one saying that seemed to fit into this horse stealing like a charm. They used to say, down there, "Follow your ore, even if it climbs a tree." That was common sense. He'd follow those horses if they went to hell. That was a darned sight better sense than guessing they'd try to cross the river that night. What if they didn't? What if they went somewhere else? That would leave the boys sitting on their tails, licking their chops and looking their eyes out. Big Butch, he muttered sarcastically, wasn't going to wait twenty-four hours and then drive those horses right where he'd be expected to. He might just as well bring them back and turn them into the Flying U corral. If Big Butch was half as smart as he was cracked up to be, he'd lay off the Whoop-up Trail with that bunch.

Later, because he was a fairly intelligent young man, it occurred to him that perhaps J.G. was shrewd enough to guess that Big Butch would cross at Cow Island because no one would suspect him of being that big a fool. He thought that over for a mile or more, and decided that J.G. wasn't so slow, after all. And he saw, too, that trailing those horses was exactly what Big Butch would expect the Flying U to do. He'd be looking for that. Watching for it.

But that did not turn Chip back. It made him study ways of being careful. Probably the whole gang wasn't in the raid. Both J.G. and Patsy thought there were five men driving the horses. That was just about half of Big Butch's gang, according to what Hec Grimes said. Chip wondered what the rest of them had been doing. Maybe the rest had waited to take the horses in charge and run them on out of the country—all the more reason why a fellow couldn't waste any time getting on the trail. Perhaps they wouldn't expect to be followed quite so soon.

Picking up the trail was simple enough. Up the rocky gully where the colt had been found, they had held the herd to a gallop, rushing them along to the final steep slope which they had climbed at top speed, judging from the tracks. Chip went up afoot, leading Mike, who was going to need his strength for other hard stretches of trail.

At the top they followed a ridge for half a mile or more. Along that hogback a man on horseback would show up like a steeple against the sky line. Chip walked that ridge with his hat off, keeping close alongside Mike's shoulder and feeling thankful he had not chosen a white tarp for his bed but a yellow-brown canvas that would not show dirt so badly on his trip north. Now it blended nicely with Dude's sorrel color, if any one should happen to be watching that telltale ridge. Furthermore, he kept over on the north side, as far down the precipitous slope as was safe. Shale rock and steep grassy inclines as slippery as glare ice prevented his hiding himself altogether from any one watching the crest, but he loafed along, letting the horses graze as they walked; not a very good disguise of his purpose, but the best he could manage, unless he waited for night. They might think a couple of horses had somehow lagged behind and were still following the bunch. At least, he hoped so.

One fact comforted him. They would never expect one man to follow them alone. And then he grinned to himself. "Cash Farley would," he thought with considerable satisfaction, and felt the better for it.

That hogback ridge dropped off steeply into a gulch that promised an opening into a valley of some extent. At the bottom of the declivity Chip mounted and rode on, guardedly and yet without loss of time. The horse herd had come this way, and the feeling persisted that the rustlers would not be looking for men on their trail so soon. Six hours' lead, they must have. They wouldn't stop yet. At that moment they might be forty or fifty miles away. They weren't the kind to save horseflesh. Still, they'd have to stop somewhere and let the horses graze; in some crooked rancher's pasture, maybe.

At dusk Chip staked his horses in a small grassy coulee, ate two biscuits and a piece of beef for his supper, lay flat on his belly and drank from a pool in a half-dried creek, and carried his outfit into a willow thicket for the night. He hated to take the time for sleep, but after two long days and a night without rest even his strong young body rebelled. Anyway, the horses had to eat and get some rest; they weren't machines, any more than he was.

Rolled in the blanket and tarp, with a flap over his head to keep bugs and mosquitoes away, he slept like a dead man through the night. Just before dawn, he awoke and cooked his breakfast over a small fire of dried willow branches. He was not much afraid of being discovered. The coulee walls were too rugged, the surrounding rim a mass of small jagged pinnacles backed by high, barren hills. No one would be coming behind, the way he had entered through a steep narrow pass, guided only by the sign of the herd he was following. And the open end, half a mile farther on, he could see from where he sat.

That day he rode warily through a wild confusion of narrow gorges dug through the ages between water-worn cliffs and small craggy hills—the Badlands of which men spoke as a place of mystery and perils unknown. Somewhere in this mad chaos Big Butch had his hideout. It might be in the next canyon, for all Chip knew. Some of the gang might be watching him now. Any turn in the steep-walled ravines might prove a trap. Any moment bring a bullet crashing into his lean hard body, seconds before the sound of the shot could reach his ears.

Yet he went on, his rifle lying across the saddle in front of him, chamber loaded, ready for instant use. His frowning eyes scanned each rock and bush before him, watched the ground for any fresh, betraying tracks. Once a grizzly appeared suddenly before him, coming out of a brush-choked gully on the left. Mike squatted in terror, Dude pulled back on the lead rope, snorting in panic. But Chip held them quiet, talking to them in a low voice. "Steady, boys—wait and see what he does. Time enough—take it easy, boys."

They stood trembling while the bear rose on his haunches and looked them over, paws drooping over his shaggy chest. He was full of wild currants, half-ripe service berries, and on his way to some fresh patch he had in mind; ready to do battle but not in the mood to start trouble. An interminable time he debated the matter within himself, then decided that he would have the berries in preference to a fight. He dropped to all fours, rumbled a warning and ambled off into a gully that opened to the right.

Chip waited until all sounds of him had ceased, then went along as if nothing had happened, though his throat had tightened while the grizzly stood there disputing the way. It was the first he had ever seen out in the open like that, and it had looked to him as big as an elephant.

Soon after that a storm struck suddenly with crash and roll of thunder and the ripping of forked lightning zig-zagging through the green-slate clouds rolling along the high peaks. Bolts struck in the canyon he was following. The air was heavy with the smell of brimstone.

Again the horses were frightened, cowering beneath the fury of the storm, but Chip merely paused long enough to button himself into his slicker and pull his big hat down to his straight eyebrows, and again urged them forward. They might as well keep right on plugging along, he told them grimly.

Though the tracks were completely obliterated under the sluicing downpour, he could still follow the sign of the herd. There were no other stock ranging in here, so far as he had discovered; it was too rough and the grassy bottoms were too few and too small. He thought the outlaws were merely taking a short cut to the country beyond, hoping to throw off any pursuit before they struck range country where grazing horse herds would confuse the trail.

Down that canyon, into another, twisting and turning deeper and deeper into the maze. The heavier lightning-charged clouds swept on eastward. For an hour or two rain fell steadily, then the drops became large and infrequent. The late sun shone dazzlingly over the drenched chaos as the strip of blue sky widened in the west—promise of a clear sunset and the moon to guide him on. So long as he could see the rain-soaked droppings of the herd, he would go on by moonlight. He hadn't pushed the horses hard today. Since noon he had been riding Dude, and at dusk he'd throw the saddle on Mike again. And at the next grass he'd stop and let them fill up while he slept. He didn't know for certain, but he thought he must have shortened the distance between himself and the stolen herd.

He was picking his way along a narrow, boxlike ravine that showed signs of pinching in, like the neck of a bottle, a mile or two ahead. He was wondering whether it would open out beyond to another of those hidden meadows where he ought to camp for a few hours, when suddenly, out around a low shoulder of rock, there came a clear, sonorous whinny. The voice of Silvia calling to her colt!

20. Chip Makes a Haul

THEY CAME CLATTERING UP THE GORGE, SILVIA AND Rummy, good old Jeff who would follow those two to China and back, all the wild broomtails; or nearly all. Twenty-five or thirty, anyway. These halted snorting, alarmed at seeing a rider, thinking themselves trapped. Chip immediately swung down, hid himself behind a boulder with the bridle reins in his hand. He did not propose to have them stampede his saddle horses and leave him afoot down there, and he did not want them turning back. He held his breath, not daring to look, except as he could peer with one eye through a crevice.

Mike whinnied hello to Jeff and Silvia. They came on, limping a little, favoring certain tender feet on the rocks. Chip had not thought of their being barefooted, and now he grinned with an ironic satisfaction. For summer pasture, practically every horse in the herd had had his shoes pulled, except the bronchos which had not yet been shod, and this was no country for a barefooted horse accustomed to springy sod. Big Butch's gang would find themselves with a bunch of lame horses on their hands, if they weren't careful.

Silvia saw friend Mike standing there waiting, and swung over. Rummy, however, was going somewhere, and he had no time to stop and visit. The range horses, always interested in colts, followed him as he galloped past. Silvia perhaps would have gone on with them, but Chip stepped out and spoke to her. She came over to him nickering, her big eyes asking where was little Silver.

The mare was in a pitiable condition, her bag swollen with milk, hard and hot to the touch. Chip talked to her, got a rope on her neck and drew out the accumulated milk, squeezing and massaging with gentle fingers. "They'd steal a good mare and then ruin her with a caked bag!" he said aloud, and added a man-sized oath for such brutality.

"All right, old girl, pull your freight and find little Silver!" he told her at last, and slipped off the rope, dismissing her with a slap on the rump. "You'll do till you get home, all right, and he'll see to it you aren't bothered with any surplus milk supply—if I know the little bum!"

With his thumbs hooked inside his chap belt, he stood and watched her go loping up the ravine, in a hurry to overtake Rummy before he got himself into trouble somehow. His eyes shone, his mouth was smiling with complacency. There went his horses, safely headed for home; a little tender-footed, but they'd get over that in the pasture.

As he swung up into the saddle and started after them, he thought of the boys waiting still at the ford. Big Butch had never intended to cross the horses there, as this eastward drive through the Badlands proved. It just went to prove that a man didn't have to be gray-headed before he could think straight. Jim Whitmore would be glad somebody else had the nerve to branch out and follow his own ideas.

No doubt it was the storm that brought these horses back, he thought. Silvia had been watching her chance, with her aching bag and her worry over her colt. When the thunder and lightning hit them, the bunch must have gone all haywire, scattering like quail. That had given Silvia her chance to break back, with Rummy and Jeff at her heels. Those broomtails were crazy about Rummy and they'd follow, but the broke horses—well, old round-up horses don't stampede so easy in a storm. They're more used to taking it as it comes. Chip would bet those rustlers had one sweet time, though . . .

Twisting his lean body in the saddle, he looked back down the narrow gorge. Those fellows never would let all these horses break back without somebody pelting after them. Even if they wouldn't take a chance on coming back, two-thirds of the Flying U herd was still missing. A pretty how-de-do, quitting at this stage of the game just because his own horses were headed for the ranch! If he ever expected to look the Flying U outfit in the face again, he'd better start in thinking of somebody beside himself. This little bunch would make it home all right—trust Silvia for that . . .

He turned and rode back again, past the place where

he had dismounted to hide lest the man-fearing bronchos bolt back the way they had come; back to the shoulder of rock that jutted out into the ravine and hid what lay beyond.

Here he heard the clink of shod hoofs striking against rock, and he reined aside into shelter where a scraggy juniper thrust out from the ledge. Shod hoofs meant a rider, some one coming after the runaways. Two, perhaps three, judging from the sound. Dude's ears tipped forward. He threw up his head to whinny, but Chip jerked it down sharply just in time; and after that the horses both stood quiet. And he waited, his heart thumping with some inner excitement which failed to reach his eyes, half shut and glittering, or his mouth, pressed into a thin, tight line.

With one hand he reached backward, fumbled beneath his pack roll and undid the buckle that closed a saddle pocket; groped swiftly inside, drew out a looped roll and tucked it inside his belt. Then again he tensed, taking quick shallow breaths, his thoughts like dragon flies darting this way and that, lacing a pattern together from disjointed phrases. What if there were more than he could handle? . . . If the boys were here, it would be pickings . . . All killers—they'd be hard to bluff . . . Cow Island was afraid of them—even Shaner . . . But if he let them go . . .

They came. Three men slowed down to a walk, riding Indian file because just here broken rock from the ledge lay scattered thick and the horses must pick their way. Three hard-bitten outlaws, and the man in the lead was Cash Farley.

Until they were free of the rocks Chip watched them over the barrel of his gun. Then, with abrupt incisiveness, he spoke. "Stop right there—and don't turn around. Hands up!"

They stiffened as if ice had been dropped down their backs but they stopped, and they were extremely careful not to turn their heads. Killers themselves, they read death in that tone.

This much was easy. The next step was going to be pretty ticklish, as Chip knew well enough without being told. He started forward, letting Mike's lead rope slide and drop to the ground, though habit brought the horse forward a step or two, his feet clattering in the loose rocks. Without turning his eyes away from the three, he spoke again. "You stay here, Mike."

He had not planned to mislead them, but he saw the three pairs of arms inch higher at the words and a wave of relief swept through his mind. They thought that second horse they heard bore a rider, and that the rider's name was Mike! He could have yelled his gratification over the mistake that solved his biggest problem.

"Hold 'em, Mike. I'll get their artillery. You plug the first son of a sea-cook that wiggles a finger." And he rode forward boldly. "Don't try to pick these up now—we'll get 'em later on."

They might have wondered why Mike did not answer; but they heard the rocks rattle back there as he shifted his feet uneasily. That proved the speaker was not alone, and it was no time to question a man's silence. They had other things to think about, anyway.

Chip worked fast. He had to. He rode up alongside

the nearest man, flipped his guns back toward the juniper, and with his own gun tucked inside his belt he yanked the fellow's hands down behind him and tied them with a double half-hitch, taking an extra turn for good measure. Then he felt for a shoulder gun, got it and threw it back with the others. He went on to the next, while the tied man cursed him bitterly.

"Keep your hands up, Farley," he warned, while he disarmed this sweating individual and tied him with a saddle string sliced off with his hunting knife—saving his second piggin string for Cash, who might need lightning work. "Mike never missed anything with a 30-30 in his life, that I know of."

"Damn you—" gritted Farley, as he felt his guns go. "I'll make you eat your own liver for this!"

"Not if Mike pinches down on that trigger, you won't," Chip told him laconically, and anchored Farley's bound wrists to the saddle as an extra precaution, using a pair of saddle strings dangling down behind the cantle. This was such a bright idea that he turned back and served the other two captives the same way before he went on to gather up the guns.

"All right, Mike, I guess you can come on," he called. And Mike came walking thankfully up to his master. "We're going to have quite a string," he remarked, emptying the revolvers and frowning over their disposal until he decided to roll them inside his pack; which he proceeded to do with his usual methodical neatness.

Left unrestrained, Cash Farley's horse moved restlessly and turned halfway around. Cash looked and saw. His face became suddenly convulsed with rage. "Well, blast my soul to hell! It's another trick of that damned Bennett kid!" he choked. "Damn you, Eb, couldn't you see what he was up to? You was closest."

Eb leaned and looked behind him and his mouth opened with blank amazement. "Hell, how was I to know?" he gasped finally. "I seen him tyin' you boys up bold as brass, no more guns than if he was wrasslin' calves—how was I to know he was holdin' us up with a pack hoss?"

"Bound t' be some more of the bunch around some-wheres," the second man—whose name later was heard as Idaho—declared in defense of his partner. "He couldn't pull off nothin' like this by his high lonesome. That," he added positively, "takes gall."

Farley's angry eyes swept the gorge on either hand. They came to rest upon Chip, who was tying the last knot on his pack roll—now considerably heavier than it had been. "Couldn't, ay? Damn 'im, he's got the gall fer anything."

Chip came forward again, leading his horse. He had a problem on his hands and he didn't quite know how he was going to handle it. But the first and most important factor was to keep those fellows helpless and on their horses, so he made the rounds and with strings sliced lavishly off their saddles he tied their legs to their stirrup leathers. Cash Farley tried to kick him in the head when he stooped to pick up a string he had dropped, but Chip dodged in time and retaliated by sticking Cash in the leg with his knife. So there was nothing more than profanity to contend with after that.

184

One thing helped considerably. The three were riding quiet, well-broken horses. Chip guessed that outlaws couldn't afford to have flighty highstrung broncs on their hands when they started out to do their dirty work. They needed mounts they could depend on not to run away, nor to jump when a gun went off suddenly in their immediate vicinity. It made it easier for him now. He simply tied them head to tail and proceeded on his way, closing his ears to the things their riders said of him.

It worried him because he did not feel equal now to going after those other horses; but he didn't see how he could manage it now, with these fellows on his hands. He had to get them to the ranch as soon as he could, because he must keep them in their saddles until he had help. He wouldn't dare let them on the ground, for he might not get them back again on their horses. He didn't know what they could do, but they were three to one and they knew all kinds of tricks, he supposed. They'd gang him sure if they saw the slimmest kind of a chance to get him. They knew darned well that he wouldn't shoot a man unless he had to.

Riding ahead of them, looking very stiff in the neck and sure of himself, Chip felt weak and trembling at the chance he had taken of getting killed. Three hard eggs like that—if any one of them had risked a glance behind him, Chip wouldn't have found it so easy. And the thought that rode him hardest was that if he had been killed, they would have got the horses back. He was human enough to shiver for the fate of Silvia and Rummy and Jeff, and not to think so much about the others. They were just horses; they could be replaced. Silvia and Rummy were like humans; any fool could see they were altogether different.

The sun sent a flaming glory upon the sullen clouds. Black with hate, spewing vileness from their malevolent minds, the three bound outlaws rode for a minute or two up a canyon bathed in an unearthly radiance. Looking back at them, Chip wondered how they could ride blindly through beauty like that, seeing nothing save new and horrible ways of murdering him when their luck turned.

They seemed so certain that the chance would come to them, he felt uncomfortable pricklings under his scalp. He wondered if they really counted on the rest of their gang turning back to overtake them. With more than fifty good saddle horses in their possession, that did not seem likely. Maybe Cash Farley, whose voice was loudest and most incessant, was only trying to scare him. Though what Cash expected to gain by it, he did not know.

The long twilight laid blankets of purple shadows in the canyons. Silvia and her following were far ahead, out of sight and hearing long ago. Perhaps when they struck the ranch, some of the boys would ride out to meet him, thinking he was bringing the rest of the herd. He hoped so. Then he could ride behind these three and be rid of that feeling of knives in his back. Couldn't drive them ahead of him now, though. They knew this country so much better than he did, they'd be sure to take a wrong turn and lose him if they could. He wasn't fool enough to give them that kind of an opening. He'd just keep plugging along the way he had come. He had the tracks to guide him and even if he lost them, his horses knew the way.

And then Chip made a very grave mistake. Instead of changing horses as he had intended to do, and riding Mike again, he kept on as he was. Dude's back was much better, and he hated to take the time necessary to shift the saddle and blanket pack. He was afraid those other fellows might take a notion to come back and help these three. They might, if they had a pasture or corral where they could throw the bunch they were driving. Dude could stand it all right, the rate they were traveling. They'd make it home by daylight, anyway.

So he kept on, while the dusk brightened to moonlight and the tumbled hills looked unreal, as if they were painted on purple velvet. There were moments when his artist eyes feasted upon the wild grandeur of the scene and he left Dude to pick his trail.

He forgot that Dude had been Cash Farley's mount for months here in these Badlands. It never once occurred to him that Dude had learned well all the sinister, blind trails of the outlaws. Had he been riding Mike, Mike would have taken him back to the Flying U corral. But Dude had learned to call another place home.

At a point where three canyons branched like spread fingers before them, Chip turned in his saddle and looked back as he rode. Looked at the droop-shouldered sullen outlaws humped in their saddles, heads bowed, silent for the moment. Looked, and lifted his eyes to a somber pinnacle that in the shadows bore star-

187

tling resemblance to a turreted castle, with one lighted slit of a window high up in a tower.

He should have stopped the cavalcade to do his gazing. But he did not, and so Dude turned calmly into a canyon which he seemed to know, and went forward steadily, with never a questioning glance to right or left. And Chip faced forward and saw nothing amiss, since all canyons looked much the same in that tricky light.

But Cash Farley lifted his head for a quick glance around—then turned in his saddle and looked back at his fellows, jerking his head in a significant gesture; whereupon they nodded to show they understood, and the third man laughed one harsh, mirthless chuckle and smothered the sound in his dirty beard.

For Dude knew that canyon of old and thought this was the way Chip wanted to go. It led, with certain devious twists and blind turnings, to Big Butch's hide-out and to the corral which Dude called home.

21. Dangerous Trails

A CERTAIN SHARP-POINTED LITTLE HILL SHOULD HAVE appeared before them, and it did not. The way they had come that morning, they had made almost a complete circuit of the odd knoll, because it had blocked the tip of a chasm nothing but a bird could cross. The way around had led through a sandy draw where the rains and snows of centuries had run down the steep hillside and sluiced a channel through to lower ground where the greedy sand had drunk it all. It was beside that knoll that Chip had changed horses at noon and had eaten the

188

last of his biscuits and beef. He remembered the place perfectly because of its odd formation, like a moat dug round a castle wall.

He began to study the hills around him, standing sharp and clear in the white moonlight. Somehow they did not seem right; look where he would, nothing seemed familiar—and yet in that grotesque confusion of hills set all askew toward one another, and of canyons and deep gorges and chasms running in all directions, there was, after all, a certain sameness to the chaotic mass left here to sag and crack and cool as it would in some primordial convulsion of the earth. The moonlight, too, with its sharp black shadows, made a difference.

Yet the sharp little hill there was no mistaking. They should have passed it long ago. He remembered now how the man called Idaho had laughed out suddenly and checked himself in the middle of it, though no one had said anything to cause that brief cackle of mirth— or to silence it, for that matter. They had been mighty quiet lately; too quiet to be natural. Chip did not like it. That chill prickling at the back of his scalp was like a friend's elbow nudging him to attention, telling him something was wrong; he had somehow missed the tracks.

But his horse seemed sure of the way. . . . And then he remembered something that made his breath stick in his throat. He remembered that Cash Farley had been riding Dude, probably for months, and that Dude had only a couple of hours' acquaintance with the Flying U corral. He wouldn't go back there of his own accord, nor would he follow Silvia and Rummy and Jeff. He had had more than two years in which to forget them. Why, these horses the outlaws were riding were old friends of Dude's.

Chip glanced behind him. Caught off his guard, Cash Farley's face in the moonlight wore a malicious, sneering grin. And like shouted words Chip read the meaning in that look. Cash Farley was waiting, gloating over the way Chip had let that sorrel have his head; grinning because he himself could not have planned better.

Chip jerked his horse to a stand, dismounted and anchored Mike to a rock. He rode back to Farley with a face like flint, twitched off the man's handkerchief and gagged him with it, stopping in the middle Cash's angry protest. Then he pulled up beside Eb. "One yip out of either one of you and I'll knock you cold," he said brusquely, and tapped his gun to make the meaning clearer. And he proceeded to gag Eb, who swore at him viciously so long as he could speak.

Idaho cringed before his implacable approach. "What's eatin' on yuh, feller? Me, I ain't spoke a word fer more'n an hour! You got no call to pick on me—I ain't said a thing!"

Until he was through and ready to start on, Chip made no remark whatever. Then he looked back along the mute line and gave a snort. "I always like to know the reason for things," he told them, in his most sarcastic tone. "Now I know one reason, anyway, why you fellows are keeping so damned quiet. And if you change your minds and want to holler your heads off, I know

190

damned good and well why you don't."

While they pondered that, glaring at him with impotent hate, he shifted his saddle to Mike, barely restraining himself from taking out his spite on Dude for getting him into this fix. Anyway, it was his own fault. He'd no business getting so worked up and excited over nabbing these fellows that he forgot he wasn't out of the woods yet, by a long shot. He'd acted like a damned pilgrim, and the sooner he came out of his trance and used his head, the better. No telling where he was, now. He might be right on top of Big Butch's camp, for all he knew.

As a matter of fact, he was within a mile of it, but it was perhaps just as well he didn't know it. He had trouble enough without that.

He didn't know just what it would be best to do. He could go back to where he had let Dude leave the trail of the horses, but he had no very clear idea of the distance, and there was the risk of meeting more of the gang. Moreover, with the cloud patches drifting up from the west again, the moonlight was tricky and there was a probability of being left in the dark altogether. In country like this, he would then have to stop and wait for morning. Of course, Mike would probably know the way home—but he was in no mood to trust himself to a horse again that night. Not altogether.

He went on across the flat they were crossing, and in spite of what he had just been telling himself, he did give Mike his head, but with his whole mind alert and watching directions. So, where Dude would have edged off to the south and entered a sandy gulch which opened a wide mouth to the flat, Mike kept on up the flat to its very end, leaving it only when he must and choosing a somewhat steep and rocky ravine that presently tilted down toward the southwest and later debouched upon another small basin which seemed sparsely covered with sagebrush.

For ten minutes then they went in darkness and Chip was bound to trust the horse whether he would or no. And when the moon emerged again, Chip saw that they were entering another gulch much like the last, but twisting and turning, yet always coming back to the same general direction, which was toward the southwest. The Whoop-up Trail lay off that way—how far off he could not tell—and it was certain Mike was traveling toward it as straight as he could go in such a rough country.

After a little Chip dismounted and walked back to see how his prisoners were coming along. He had an uneasy feeling that this journey was altogether too tame and peaceful to be trusted; as if they were somehow going to work loose and escape or something, though he didn't see how they could. Their eyes were murderous, but their bonds were as he had tied them. There was nothing they could do save sit in their saddles and ride wherever he led the way. So he berated himself for being skittish over nothing, and mounted and rode on again, letting Mike find his own trail.

It was with a distinct feeling of relief that he rode out of a dry sandy wash into a long narrow valley lying peaceful under the moon, its close rim of hills oddly familiar. Mike knew it, too—Chip sensed that at once by the way his ears stood forward and he felt for the bit, thrusting out his nose for more slack in his reins as his pace quickened. As his feet struck into a dim trail through the grass, he heaved a sigh as horses will, and started to lope forward; but the jerk on his tail stopped that and he decided that a trot would do.

This was the place where Chip had held up Cash Farley and taken Dude away from him. He couldn't resist the temptation to turn and look at Cash, though the light was failing again and he could not see much of his face. Cash was remembering all about it; that was a cinch. Maybe he was seeing that a man didn't have to go around shooting and killing in order to hold his own in this world. Chip hoped so. He also hoped that Hec Grimes would learn a lesson from this capture and would admit that brains were better than bullets any day. Here he was, hadn't fired a shot at a man in his whole life, and look what he'd managed to do! Caught Cash Farley cold, twice hand running—to say nothing of these other two jaspers that were probably killers.

With these thoughts and others quite as self-satisfied, Chip rode steadily toward the moon and the Missouri River. Since they struck the trail, they were making better time and he had no further worry. Not far ahead now was the creek they must follow; then they would be in the road, and a few miles more would land them in Cow Island. They'd open their eyes, Burch and Shaner and all of them, when he turned over three of Big Butch's gang—that they were all so scared of!

He was approaching the creek, riding along the south wall of the valley, when Mike suddenly threw up his head and took mincing steps, staring toward the hidden stream. And Chip, who knew every mood and every movement of the horse, swung out of the trail and into the black shadow of the cliff. As surely as though Mike had spoken, he knew that some one was coming in from the main road; some one he was certain he would not want to meet, since this was not a trail known to many.

To swerve from the trail and ride in behind a line of brush next the cliff was too instinctive an action to be called a decision. He had to hide in a hurry. He knew that. The next instant he was off his horse, darting from horse to horse, ruthlessly slicing saddle strings and tying them around the nose of each horse, so there could be no whinny nor even a snort to betray him. He stepped up close to Cash Farley, standing so that he faced the other two.

"I'll kill the man that makes a sound," he hissed fiercely, and pulled his gun and stepped back so that, while almost within reach, he still could shoot at any one of the three and be sure of hitting his mark.

His heart pounded like slow hammer beats while he waited—and though it seemed long, it must have been a matter of seconds that he listened to the measured splashing of wading horses. Then a rider tilted up into sight over the bank and came on in white moonlight. Big Butch, looming huge in the saddle, his long blond mustache standing out crisply on either side of his florid face, his light eyes gleaming like a cat's as the moon shone full upon him. Big Butch and three of his men, coming straight toward him as if they knew he was there at bay against the cliff.

22. "The Charge Is Horse-Stealing!"

CHIP HELD HIS BREATH, AFRAID TO LOOSE IT LEST BIG Butch hear it, he came so close. Then the trail bent away from the cliff toward the open flat, and their faces were turned a little from the bushes. He wished they would talk; the silence was so profound he feared the breathing of the horses standing there.

Then Cash Farley took a chance and kicked his horse, making it start forward, rattling the branches of the bush where he stood. But there again Chip's guardian angel was alert, for a breeze swooped down into the basin and set all the bushes swaying, and Chip had reached out and caught the horse, shoving his gun barrel hard into Cash's belly.

Dust was lifted in the trail. One of the horses out there sneezed.

"Betcha it'll rain b'fore mornin'," the last man said listlessly.

Big Butch turned in his saddle, cast a glance up and around, sweeping the sky with its drifting clouds and dropping his gaze to the surrounding hills. Had he known exactly where Chip and his prisoners were concealed, he could not have looked straighter at them. Yet in the black shadows he saw nothing.

"Ain't liable to," he said. "Not this far down. Like t'-day, they never got a sprinkle at Cow Island, ner this far north."

The man next behind him laughed. "Wel-l, lay the dust and yuh leave tracks like a duck in a mud puddle," he remarked. "You pays your money and you takes your choice."

"Not me, I don't," Big Butch retorted. "I takes my choice but I don't pay no money."

His three companions laughed at that, evidently applying the remark humorously to some recent transaction. Running off the Flying U horses, Chip thought bitterly. Butch's horse felt a sting of the spurs and broke into a gallop, the others following. They loped off down the trail, their forms blurring in the dust they made.

As he made his way to where Mike stood at the end of the line, Chip staggered a little. He was yet too young to take these close calls as a matter of course, or perhaps he had too much imagination. All he could think of just then was the disaster that would have befallen him had he been three minutes sooner or later along that trail. A little sooner, he would have met Big Butch face to face in the creek channel. It didn't require much imagination to guess what would have happened then. He was no gunman and he never would be one. Big Butch would have killed him, then or back in the open. Either way, he had missed death by too small a margin for steady nerves. He was so shaken that he almost forgot to take those strings off the horses' noses before he started on.

It was a strange cavalcade that forded the river that night. Turk Bowles, coming to the door of his shack when he heard the splashing in the river, gobbled an excited sentence that brought Hec Grimes to the doorway, five cards in his hand. His eyes were popping when he turned back and flung down the cards. "I gotta go, Turk. That there was the Bennett boy leadin' Cash Farley an'—my Gawd, he'll git himself killed for shore! Ain't got no more sense than a last year's bird's-nest, when it comes to keepin' his fingers outa the fire."

What Turk said cannot be written intelligibly, but its meaning was a general agreement with Hec, who was trotting up the road to the settlement, talking to himself as he went.

Barr Lang was pouring himself a big glass of beer as a night-cap while the bartender got ready to lock up. Across the way, Dave Burch's light went out as Chip pulled up at the hitch rail and went into the saloon. Lang looked up, stared and came forward. "The Bennett boy, ain't yuh? What's the matter? Anything wrong out at the Flying U?" He looked at his stein of beer, set it back on the bar without drinking. "The boys left this afternoon," he added, as if that might help.

Chip stood within the doorway, glancing sharply from Lang to the bartender and back. The pupils of his eyes were like pinheads, giving him a fierce intent look. "I've got three men out here I want to turn over to whatever law you've got in this burg," he said bluntly. "Horse thieves. Some of the gang that raided the Flying U."

"What's that? Who—"

"Cash Farley and two more. What'll I do with 'em?"

Lang crooked a finger at the bartender as he came forward. "Charley, you run across and get Dave and Tom." He stared at Chip doubtingly. "Cash Farley? You sure?"

"I ought to be."

"Well—who's with you?" Lang peered out of the

open door and stepped back as if he had seen something he shouldn't.

"Nobody but those three." Chip turned and glanced outside. "They can't make a break. I've got 'em tied on."

"I'll—be—damned!" breathed Lang, just above a whisper. "You done it alone? How in hell—"

"I'll tell all that at the trial," Chip cut him off. "Say, Mr. Lang, is it too late to get a little something to eat?" His tone and manner relaxed a little under Barr Lang's very human surprise and sympathy. "I haven't had any supper," he explained simply.

Lang looked at the big round-faced clock on the wall, looked again at Chip. "It's after one o'clock," he said unnecessarily. "I'll see if I can scare up something. Want a bed too, don't you?"

Of a sudden Chip knew that he was dog tired, and that a bed under the same roof with his Goldilocks would be like going to heaven. But there were his horses. "I've got an outfit," he said. "I'll sleep outside. But I sure would like some supper if I can get it."

Lang walked lumbering to a doorway, disappeared for a minute or two and came back, hurrying as though he feared he might miss something. Chip was still waiting in the saloon, half sitting on a card table, shaking tobacco into a cigarette paper and spilling more than he saved, his fingers shook so. Lang's little eyes in their rolls of fat noticed that and flicked up to study Chip's face. He looked fagged, years older than he had been the Fourth.

"Beats me," said Lang. "Anybody but Cash Farley—"

Chip was drawing the tobacco bag shut, one end of the string caught between his teeth. The operation gave him a grinning look which his bleak eyes contradicted. "Cash Farley don't like the idea of a bullet in his back, any more than any one else," he said, and walked to the door, rolling the cigarette as he went.

In the doorway he dropped it and whipped out his gun, firing at something outside.

"Hey! Get away from those prisoners!" he yelled. "What the hell do you think you're doing?" He shot again, aiming low so that the bullet spatted into the ground ten feet short. There was an answering flash, the bullet kicking bark against Chip's cheek. A man running toward the corner of the dance hall turned and fired another shot before he disappeared around the corner.

Chip ran that way, hugging the wall. Men were running across from the blacksmith shop and the stable, but Chip was only vaguely aware of them. He reached the corner, edged around it carefully, with his gun pointing the way. There was nothing. In the shadows of the grove, dry twigs were cracking, and that was all. He had no mind to go man-hunting in that brush at night, so he turned back and came face to face with Dave Burch.

"What's all this? What's all this shooting about?" Burch demanded, the harsh note of authority in his tone.

"Some damned busybody thought he'd turn these prisoners loose." Chip ran past Burch, coming to a stop beside Cash Farley. The gag was off, pulled down around Farley's neck. His hands were loose—but he was still anchored to the saddle and he was snarling like a trapped wolf.

"Drop that knife, you—!" cried Chip, "before I hand you the hot end of a bullet! . . . Drop it!"

Cash dropped it, cursing and spitting at the taste of the knotted corners of his own dirty neckerchief he had been obliged to chew on for hours. "I'll skin you alive for this," he promised savagely.

"Oh, I don't know," drawled Chip, stepping aside as Burch shouldered his way to the man's side. "According to my experience, Cow Island isn't so friendly to horse thieves. You won't be skinning anything except your teeth, when the rope tightens."

"What's the charge against these men? Who brought 'em in? You?" Burch spoke irritably, as if he found his official duties somewhat onerous at this time of night and when some one else thrust them upon him.

"There ain't any charge," Cash Farley said quickly, with profane trimmings. "That damned half-wit there held us up—"

"The charge," Chip cut in sharply, "is horse-stealing. I brought 'em in, and if you love law and order the way you claim you do, you'll lock 'em up till you can get your jury together."

"I don't need to be told what to do," Dave Burch squelched him. "Tom, you and Jim and Wallace take these men in charge. I'll hold you responsible for their appearance at nine o'clock tomorrow morning. You," he barked, stabbing a finger toward Chip, "come over to my office and swear out your complaint, and name your witnesses."

"If it's a horse thief you're lookin' for, grab that fool," Cash Farley sneered. "He stole that sorrel from me the Fourth."

"That's a lie!" Chip retorted angrily. "I took back the horse you stole from my brother. Jim Whitmore can swear to that."

A throaty chuckle from the saloon porch interrupted. "Kinda jeopardizin' your reputation, ain't yuh, Cash? Seems to me the kid there has kinda got you buffaloed." Barr Lang laughed again.

"I ain't through with him yet," Cash growled. "You wait till the last card's turned. He ain't got the brains of a louse—layin' in the brush and holdin' up folks that's just ridin' along the trail! Burch, you got no license to hold us here. Turn us loose er we'll tear this damn place apart."

Burch turned to him with a pacific gesture. "Now, now, Mr. Farley, you know the law laid down by our Committee. Every man brought before us has got to be tried, whether er no. Tom'll take yuh over and make yuh comf'table till morning, and the trial'll show up the facts. If you want to call in any witnesses—"

"Hell, I don't need no witnesses!" snorted Farley. "There ain't no case. That damn idiot there thinks he's a Billy the Kid er somebuddy—"

"Well, well, it'll all come out at the trial," Burch repeated nervously. "You take 'em over to your place, Tom, and keep 'em till morning." He turned and beckoned Chip to follow.

"What are you so polite about?" Chip called out reck-

201

lessly to Shaner, who was trying to placate Farley as he led the three across to the stable. "Why don't you knock him in the head with an ax or something, the way you did me?" He gave a hard, mirthless laugh. "Hell, I didn't know you said it with flowers. I always supposed it was a pick handle you used!"

That stirred up language, but Chip didn't care. He was willing at that moment to fight the pack of them. Knuckling down like that to Cash Farley—why didn't they give him that potato pile to sleep on? He certainly had it coming, and so did the rest of them. They must be awful scared of these birds,—and at the thought his lip curled with contempt. They might be tough, but they sure gentled down nice as anybody when you poked a six-gun at them.

Vaguely uneasy, more disheartened than he would have admitted even to himself, he ate a cold supper which Barr Lang himself set out for him, took his horses down to the camp ground where two freight out-fits were camped for the night, and having foraged for hay enough for Dude and Mike, he rolled himself in his blanket and slept. But his dreams were troubled ones in which he fought over and over a desperately one-sided battle with Big Butch's gang. He thought he was trying to kill Cash Farley—did kill him, more than once. But always when he thought the fight was over, there was Cash coming at him again; a man who wouldn't stay dead.

23. Cow Island Justice

IN THE BLACKSMITH SHOP A DOZEN MEN WERE ASSEM-
bled, the smoke-tainted gloom of the big building in
sharp contrast with the hot glare of the mid-morning
sun outside. Cash Farley and his two companions sat
unbound, in a row upon the beam of a heavy old plow
with rusted share. Hats on the backs of their heads, they
were smoking and listening to the evidence against
them which, when it lay pared down to the bare bone of
facts, looked pretty thin. Cash was grinning maliciously
at the stubborn truthfulness of Chip's testimony.

"You say you didn't see these men take the horses?"

"No. They took them about the time we left here to go
back to the ranch."

"Who did see them take the horses out of the Flyin' U
pasture?" Dave Burch was being very exact, very
careful of the perfect justice of his questions. Chip had
to concede that.

"Well, Mr. Whitmore fired some shots at them as they
went past the camp, and Patsy the cook fired his
shotgun."

"Did they hit any of the thieves?".

"Well, they didn't know for sure. J.G. thought he did,
but they were too far off to be certain."

"Hmm. They was too far off to tell whether he hit any
one. How did he reckanize these men? Was they closer,
before he started in shootin'?"

Chip felt a premonitory sinking of a weight in his
chest. "N-no, I don't believe they were. He woke up

and ran out as they were going past with the horses." And he foresaw the next question, foresaw too that he could not answer it satisfactorily.

"How did he know it was these men, then?"

And the inevitable answer, "He said he was pretty sure it was Big Butch's gang."

The captain of the Vigilance Committee gave a snort which Chip knew was justified. "That there is no evidence at all," he complained. "You couldn't hang a side uh pork on that kinda evidence."

"No, sir, it isn't proof," Chip admitted.

"Well, then *did* you see these fellers drivin' the Flyin' U horses, then?"

Chip chose his words carefully. "Well, I was following the tracks through the Badlands yesterday afternoon. There was a pretty hard storm, with lots of thunder and lightning, and some of the horses broke back on them and started home. My mare's colt was back at the ranch and she was crazy to get to it. A lot of the horses followed her and I met them."

"Was these men with them?"

"No. They hadn't caught up with them. I caught the mare and milked her out, and then started her home. And I went on—I started on, I mean—to try and get the rest of the horses."

"Well, where did you see these men? Was they driving the rest of the herd?"

"No," said Chip, "they weren't. They were coming after the bunch that got away. I met them in the canyon. I heard them coming, on around a turn, so I pulled out to one side behind a bush—a juniper—and waited till they got past. Then I threw down on them." He glanced at Cash. "And brought them in," he added with a pardonable satisfaction.

Burch lifted his heavy, iron-gray brows and looked from witness to prisoners. If he thought it a large order for the young fellow before him, he did not say so. He stuck very close to the salient points.

"How long was it after the horses come along before these men showed up?"

Chip flushed and bit his lip. "Ten or fifteen minutes. I was fussing with the mare that long, I guess."

Captain Burch scowled. "We don't want any more guesswork. That's about all we've had, so fur," he stated glumly. "You shore it wasn't more'n fifteen minutes?"

"It wasn't much more. I'm sure of that."

"Well, you heard these men say they was comin' home from the Larb Hills country and was takin' a short cut. Can you swear they was after your horses?"

"I'd swear to it, yes. I know they were. Maybe I couldn't prove it, though."

"Is there anything," Captain Burch asked dryly, "that you *can* prove?"

"Well," Chip retorted in the same tone, "I can prove what I think of the bunch. I brought them in here and turned them over to you—and that proves I know in my own mind they're guilty as hell." He turned and gave the three a long, deliberate stare. "I proved to them, anyway, that I'm dead next to them. They stole those horses, and if they get away with it, they're just lucky, that's all."

205

"We ain't here to prove your opinion of them or any-buddy else," Burch told him with his most judicial tone and manner. "We got to have facts, not opinions. If that's all you can prove, I guess we're through takin' your testimony."

"Yes, Sir," Chip answered that crisply, and went to the doorway, standing there leaning against the grimy casing while he made himself a smoke. Since he was the accuser, they had questioned him first. Now Cash Farley was being called to stand before Burch.

Sick at heart, Chip turned away. He felt that he could not stand there and listen to what Cash Farley would say—the lies he would tell. Now that it was too late, he wished that he had taken those damned hounds to the ranch. That's what he should have done, no matter how far it was. He could have stood the ride all right, and they couldn't have helped themselves. J.G. and the boys would have known what to do with them, quick enough. He was just a damned, swell-headed fool, bringing them here to this Cow Island bunch. He might have known how it would pan out.

Hec Grimes, coming at a shambling run up the road, saw him standing there gloomily at the corner of the shop and swerved that way. With frantic gestures imploring haste and silence, he beckoned Chip to follow him around behind the coal shed.

"What's eating on yuh, Hec?" he demanded sourly, when they stood together in the rank burdock weeds.

"You come with me, Chip," Hec panted, and led the way into a junk-cluttered gully behind the buildings. "You shore are in fer it now! How's she goin'? They're turnin' Cash an' them loose, ain't they?"

"They will. Burke's going to unwind some of that red tape of his, and then the damned—will walk outa there, all set to go steal some more horses. Why? What's on your chest?"

"Come awn!" Hec urged him along faster. "Whoever it was tried t' turn them fellers loose, las' night, he musta went an' told Butch about it. Big Butch an' about six of his bunch is comin'. I seen 'em ride into the river."

"Coming as character witnesses, probably," Chip snorted. "Too bad. They're going to be late for the show. It's all over but the shouting."

In haste though he was, Hec stopped short and turned a look of deep disgust on Chip. "You damned fool," he said huskily; "it's all over but the shootin', you mean. Don't yuh know they'll kill yuh? It's twice now you've th'owed an' tied Cash Farley. Draggin' him in here t' stand trial—say, they'll kill yuh by inches fer that!"

"Oh, I guess not that bad." But the blood seeped from Chip's face and he walked a little faster.

"I knowed they'd turn them fellers loose," Hec went on hurriedly. "Them makin' the talk they done, about you not havin' no case agin 'em—and you bein' all stark solitary alone—nobuddy t' back you up in nothin'—I knowed as well as 't I'm alive 't they'd git off. It was a cinch."

"I kinda thought they would, myself."

"You'd oughta thought b'fore yuh went an' tied into that bunch," Hec complained. "Any time yuh go after any of them birds, you want to have a cinch." He stopped and jerked a thumb over his shoulder. "There they go—Butch and them. Come on, now. You wait a minute right there by the ferry. I got yore hosses tied back up here in the bushes. I saddled up for yuh. I knowed damn good an' well you'd be pullin' out in front of a flock uh bullets."

Chip slowed, stopped. "I know your intentions were fine, Hec—but, damn it, I haven't done anything—"

"Nothin' but act the cussed fool," Hec grumbled, as he went off to bring the horses.

Chip waited, but his mouth was set in stubborn lines, his eyes held rebellion. He did not mean to sneak off like a coyote when the dogs bark at dawn. Even Big Butch wouldn't dare shoot him in broad daylight, right there in Cow Island. There'd be something for the bunch to stand trial for, then. He wasn't going to run. He had to see Goldilocks before he left. It was mostly on that account he had decided to bring his prisoners here and turn them over to Burch; not to show off, as Hec seemed to think—but to furnish an excuse to see Julie. She hadn't waited on table at breakfast that morning. He had eaten at the hotel, expecting to see her. Now he had to find some other way. He certainly wasn't going to pull out now. . . .

Hec had other ideas about that. "Here yuh are," he said gruffly, when he handed Chip the reins. "Crawl that hull now, an' hightail it fer home quick as the good Lord'll let yuh. They'll have a drink er two first—"

"I'm not going," Chip told him bluntly. "I don't think I can be called a coward—yet. But—" he grinned disarmingly at Hec "—if I fan it outa here now—"

"Hell!" snapped Hec. "Stayin' here ain't courage, boy; that's plain damn ignorance!" He pulled out his plug, looked at it, waved it toward Lang's Place. "You wanta git yourself beefed, an' let that bunch fog it over to the Flyin' U and ketch 'em when they ain't lookin'? Hell, they got their honor to defend, now! They been publicly accused uh stealin' horses! An' the Flyin' U has did the accusin'. You hit fer home an' tell 'em what all you been up to—and if ole J.G. don't dust your britches for yuh, he'd oughta."

Chip looked toward Lang's, looked back at Hec. "Gosh, you don't think they'd tackle—"

"Think!" snorted Hec, almost weeping with his earnestness, "Think! Hell, man, I know!"

Without another word, Chip went into the saddle and hit the river at a lope.

24. The Shot in the Coulee

IT WAS THE MORNING OF THE FOURTH DAY AFTER CHIP'S tumultuous return. Nothing whatever had happened save a lot of useless preparations for trouble that failed to arrive, and a great deal of bunk-house argument which, having covered the ground thoroughly several times, now was forced to talk in circles. Chip was getting tired of listening to the endless discussion, though until now he hadn't said much. After tearing home and telling them to get ready for a battle, because Big Butch and his gang were coming, there didn't seem to be much left to say.

Cal Emmett came in last to breakfast and he was carrying his rifle ostentatiously over his shoulder as he dodged in and slammed the door shut behind him. With the butt of his gun he nudged Happy Jack along on the bench nearest him. "Shove over, Happy," he requested. "I gotta set here where I can aim and shoot out the window without gittin' up. I been buildin' myself a case of dyspepshy, jumpin' up every minute when some-buddy hollered Big Butch. Me, I gotta take more care of m'self from now on."

"Yep—pining away to a cart load," Penny declared, tilting his head sidewise to size Cal up the better. "Careful, boy. This strain is gittin' yuh down."

"I know it," sighed Cal, reaching a long arm to spear a slab of beefsteak the size of his foot. "My appetite's goin' back on me. I couldn't eat but 'leven slapjacks yesterday." With a wicked eye turned toward Chip, he leaned and peered through the window, one hand going out to the gun standing beside him. Then he settled back with his left hand on his heart and a look of collapse on his face. "Nope—nothin' but a' chicken hawk castin' his shadow before."

Several of the boys laughed. "Before what?" some one asked.

"Before Big Butch," Cal elaborated gravely. "Gee whiz, this strain is awful!"

Chip looked up with a bitter twist of the lips that had meant to be a smile. "Somebody knock Cal on the head and put him out of his misery," he suggested, in his most sarcastic voice. "If I'd known it was going to scare him to death, I wouldn't have said anything about Big Butch's intentions."

"You didn't," Cal told him regretfully. "It's these damn nightmares I can't stand."

"Yes?" Chip's only sign of mental disturbance was the extra spoonful of sugar he dipped into his coffee.

Shorty put an end to Cal's rough joking. Knife and fork poised over his plate, he leaned and looked down the table to where Chip sat, wanting to murder Cal. "On the square, Chip, how'd you find out Big Butch was comin' up here to clean us out? He say so?"

Chip drew a quick breath through his nostrils. It was a question he had been dreading during the past two days. But he would not hedge or deny. He sat forward so that he could return Shorty's look. "He'd be a fool if he did, wouldn't he? No, I didn't see Butch himself. Cash Farley made some cracks at that alleged trial. Bragged of what he'd do to me. Of course I expected that. When Burch began to holler for actual open-and-shut proof, I knew what was coming." To show the calmness he did not feel, he took a swallow of coffee and set down the cup neatly, in the exact center of the wet ring where it had stood.

"No," he added the complete answer to Shorty's question, "it was Hec Grimes told me. I was going to stay and have it out with Cash and be done with it, one way or the other"—lying a little there, because he would not say he was going to stay to see Julie Lang. No one knew how he felt about his Goldilocks, and they weren't going to know, either, till it was all settled and he was ready to tell them.

"But Hec raised particular hell with me. He said the whole gang would head straight for here, and if I didn't beat them to it and warn you, the Flying U would be wiped out." He gave a snort of disgust, his defiant hazel-brown eyes moving from face to face. "I realize now that it was a case of casting pearls before swine. But since some of you seem all broke up over it, I suppose I'd better apologize because that bunch didn't come and kill you off. Sorry, boys," he added, straddling the bench to rise from the table. "Hope the worst befalls you next time."

"My gosh, how I hate an edjycated guy!" groaned Cal, as Chip passed him on his way to the door. "Now I don't know whether I'm a pearl or a swine, gol darn it!"

"Go look in the glass and you can tell quick enough," Chip flung bitingly over his shoulder as he went out.

He met Patsy just outside the door with an empty milk pan and a family sized coffeepot in his hands. Patsy had been taking Jim Whitmore's breakfast in to him, using the pan in place of a tray. "Der poss vants to talk mit," he grunted, as he went by. "I pet you gid fired yoost for two cents, so you look out."

Whereupon Chip gave another snort of disdain at such narrow-mindedness. The way every one was acting, you'd think, by gosh, they were blaming him because they hadn't been killed! And now J.G. was going to tear into him about it. It made Chip tired.

Jim Whitmore was sitting in a chair with his wounded leg stretched out before him on a blanket-padded box, eating beefsteak and fried potatoes and sour-dough biscuit with an appetite that would have startled a dietitian of today into predicting an early demise for the invalid.

Ignorance being bliss in this case, however, J.G. was enjoying his breakfast with no fear that it would shorten his life. He looked up, swallowing a mouthful as Chip appeared. "Had your breakfast? Set down. I want you to give me the straight of this run-in you had with Big Butch and his gang. Looks like we've wasted four good days hangin' around the ranch here, waitin' for 'em to come and make their war talk. How about it? Where'd you git the idee they was comin' to wipe us out?"

Chip braced himself for the worst. At least, he could be thankful J.G. wasn't going to josh and bedevil him about it the way the boys had been doing, the last day or two. He had told the story before, with a becoming modesty that omitted certain colorful details of the exploit, touching mainly upon his disgust at the fear Cow Island seemed to have of offending Cash Farley and the rest. He especially dwelt upon the injustice of giving Cash Farley a bed at the livery stable, when by rights they should have suffered the lumps and the smells of that potato pile in the cellar. But he told a more circumstantial story this time, which revealed the fact that he had taken Hec Grimes' word for more than he should, perhaps.

Jim Whitmore used the last piece of his second biscuit to mop up the steak gravy on his tin plate. Until that was accomplished to his complete satisfaction, he made no comment whatever; while Chip sat smoking and absently watching the process.

"Hec Grimes ain't more'n about half-baked," Jim Whitmore observed without malice, when he had finished and was getting out his old briar pipe. "Calamity howler, from all I know of 'im. It don't look like Big Butch is goin' to take up the quarrel; don't see what he'd expect t' gain by it—and it's Number One he's always lookin' out for, you can bet on that."

"Cash Farley, and Eb and Idaho—they said—"

"Yeah; well, they're a horse of another color. They'll git back at yuh, give 'em a chance. You'll have to stick to your own range and keep outa their way. But Butch is after the almighty dollar. He ain't goin' to let them three put off up here just to settle a personal grudge with a kid. They got fifty head of broke horses to cash in on. That comes first with Butch. And he knows damn well—or would, if he took the trouble to think it out— that I can't spare the men to go git 'em back."

"I'd have gone on after them, Mr. Whitmore, only I had to grab those fellows when they came along. They'd have got the ones that did start home." Chip's voice told how far he felt he had fallen short of his full duty. "And then when—after that, I was afraid to go on after the horses. I didn't think I could handle the rest of the bunch."

Jim Whitmore was an old smoker, but he choked on a mouthful of smoke until tears came into his eyes. "You was workin' on your own time," he said gruffly, when he could trust himself to speak. "I never told yuh to tackle that job, remember. You quit and went off on your own hook. You don't have to apologize to me for not cleanin' up the hull gang."

That sounded like sarcasm. Chip turned a dark red under his tan. "I wasn't apologizing for not cleaning up the whole gang. I don't seem to have accomplished much of anything," he said stiffly, "except build up a fine large feud, maybe." He flung his half-burned cigarette spitefully outside and rose. "I realize that I made a damned fool of myself all around if that's what you're hinting at—but as you say, it seems to be my own lookout. So I'll just go on being a damned fool, trying to find out what happened to Wane, and getting his stuff back."

"*Seddown!*" roared J.G. "How many times have I got t' tell you to keep away from that river?" He sucked savagely on his pipe. "Dawgoned if I wouldn't ruther learn a bull calf t' drink out of a bucket! Short-handed as I be, d' you think I'm goin' to let you go scurrupin' around on a wild-goose chase that'll git yuh killed? If there was any way of findin' out about Wane, don't yuh s'pose I'd 'a' done it long ago? Hell, it'd take a regiment uh soldiers t' comb the country like it'd have t' be combed. Yore father was a damn good friend of mine; don't yuh s'pose I done all I could t' git at the bottom of that drowndin'?"

He glared at Chip, tamped the tobacco down in his pipe and spat. "Wane could of been workin' for me and kept outa trouble, only he wanted to be close to the river. Got stuck on that yella-headed hussy at Lang's. Had t' be close, where he could hang around there half the time. Didn't have sense enough t' see she was just playin' him for a sucker, just as she does the rest of the damn fools that hang around there. *That's* why he didn't want t' work fer me. Too fur from Cow Island—"

Chip was white now as his tan would let him be. "Mr. Whitmore—"

"Don't Mr. Whitmore me! You'll keep away from down there if I have t' hog-tie yuh. You've got 'em all after your scalp now—that'd oughta satisfy yuh fer awhile. I sh'd think," he added, dropping to his old whimsical complaining, "you'd git action enough on the broncs you'll have to help take the wire edge off of. You got a fine chance there t' git your neck broke, if that's all yuh want." He grunted and with both hands lifted his leg to a new place on the blanket.

"A busted bone ain't as painful as a bullet hole," he stated grimly. "I've sampled both, so I'd oughta know. You ramble over t' the mess house and tell Shorts I want him. And don't let me hear no more about this fool quittin'. You'll quit when I tell yuh you're fired, and not before."

Furious, yet with an unaccountable feeling of relief down deep in his heart, Chip went off to do as he was told. He could have choked J.G. till his eyes popped. Calling Julie a name like that—saying she—well, just as good as saying she was just a mean little flirt that only wanted to make a fool of a man. Chip went hot all over when he thought of it.

She wasn't like that at all. J.G. didn't know what he was talking about. Just because she was beautiful and he was too darned old to understand or appreciate a girl like that. He probably meant all right, but what did an old man of forty know about girls, anyway? A fellow just had to consider the source and forget about it.

Anyway, he still had his job. That was a bigger relief than he would admit to himself, though it carried the stinger of being forbidden to go back to the river for

216

awhile. Still, if he were slammed up in a corner and made to come clean with the truth, he would have to admit that he would just as soon stay away till things cooled down a little. Cash Farley certainly wasn't the killer folks tried to make out he was, but Chip wouldn't put it past him to try and start something, if they happened to run across each other.

And he certainly was thankful old J.G. had headed him off before he gave himself away about Julie. Had his mouth all fixed to tell the boss where he could go— it would have been a dead give-away. No, the thing to do was to make a hand here and help get another remuda shaped up for fall round-up. Then he'd make some excuse and get a few days off, and go right down to Cow Island and board at Lang's till he found out the truth about Wane, and got his stuff together. He'd have a chance then to see Goldilocks every day without advertising it to the whole country. Another month—it was going to be pretty hard to wait that long, but he couldn't see any other way out.

All this while he was riding down east of the ranch in the rough country north of the breaks, hunting horses. He had started out with Weary and Cal, the other boys riding north. But with water everywhere and plenty of good feed, the broomtails had split into small bands and mixed with other brands, so it wasn't so easy to comb them out of the draws and get them all headed in to the ranch. One little bunch of a dozen or so ducked down into a gully, and Chip went after these alone. Weary was chasing a few saddle-marked geldings up over a ridge, thinking to swing them toward the round-up ground and let them go. And Cal was off somewhere on a quest of his own and hadn't been seen by either for more than half an hour.

Chip was just as well pleased to be rid of Cal; Weary, too, for that matter. In fact, the less he saw of any of the boys the better he'd like it, until they quit chewing the rag about that false alarm of his.

The gully, deepening to a rocky gulch as it sloped downward, opened out unexpectedly into a small coulee with high walls and a narrow, grassy bottom, open country showing beyond. Already the horses he was after were racing away toward the mouth of the coulee, wheeling now and then to stare back at him for a moment before they turned and went on.

Chip was riding Dude that day, chiefly because he was a shade faster than Alike, a little quicker at turning. With four days of rest on good grass, today he was running like an antelope. He went down that coulee like a sorrel streak, gaining on the straight-away so that Chip was sure he'd have the bunch turned and headed the other way in another half mile at the most. Beyond the coulee the land sloped gently down to a creek bottom thinly wooded, the immediate slope broken into small round ridges, much like the ground swell of an ocean lazily recovering from a storm. Not bad country to ride over; better than a flat covered with prairie-dog villages. He could get into one of those swales and ride out of sight, heading the herd back up the coulee to join the bunches Weary and Cal would have on the upper flat.

He rode out of the coulee at top speed, reined toward a smooth-looking draw that seemed to run in the direction he wanted. He was just entering it, when something zipped across his thigh; and in the middle of his stride Dude faltered, tried to gather himself, then went down head foremost in a heap.

Chip heard the distant crack of a rifle as he hit the ground, by sheer instinct jerking his feet from the stirrups as he went down. And for an unmeasured space of time, that was the last he knew of anything.

25. Cash Farley Strikes

ONE CANNOT GAUGE BY ITSELF A TIME OF COMPLETE unconsciousness. Chip heard the shot as he went down. Then a blank space. Next, he was lying on the south side of the gully, his head in the shade of a tall clump of weeds. He looked at Dude and saw a round hole appear suddenly in his flank, with a soft plopping sound. Then he heard a rifle shot. He pulled in his feet with the flashing thought of how lucky he was not to be pinned under the horse.

Another hole in Dude's sweaty neck came with a swiftness that spoke of concentrated venom on the part of the shooter. They certainly didn't intend that he should escape—they were hunting him under that horse with their bullets. If he had his carbine there in its scabbard, he'd take a hand in this target practice himself. Even the way his head was buzzing, he thought he could give a pretty fair account of himself.

But he was afraid to slide down where he could reach for the gun. Dude had fallen on the other side, with the gun stock sticking up in plain sight. A good old 30-30 that had been his father's. He was afraid a bullet might smash the stock. They certainly would shoot it if they happened to see it—and then he realized that they were not close enough to see the gun. If they were, they'd know he was not there—pinned underneath. It must be he they were trying to get; they wouldn't waste bullets on a dead horse. By "they," he of course meant Cash Farley and Eb and Idaho; perhaps the rest of the gang as well. There was no doubt of that, nor that Cash had recognized him at a distance by the horse he rode. He'd know Dude as far as he could see him.

Never in his life had Chip been so scared. Never had he felt more helpless, more alone—unless it was while he lay in that root cellar. He had to have that carbine, but for all it was so close, it might as well have been across the ridge, he thought desperately. As it was, he was barely hidden. Only for this clump of weeds—wild sunflowers, they were—he might be in plain sight of them. From the sound of the shots, they must be up on the coulee rim. On their way to the ranch, he guessed, coming in from a direction that would put them on the north rim of Flying U Coulee. Lord, they could lie up there and shoot right down on the camp!

But that was still in the future. Now, he had to save his life, if he could. He started crawling down the gully, flattening his body to earth, thankful for the fringe of tall grass and weeds, yet afraid that they would not extend far enough. He had gained a few yards when he came up against a scraggy sage bush that halted him. If he crawled down into the bottom of the gully to get around the bush, he would probably be seen and shot.

If he crawled up the bank, they couldn't miss seeing him. He thought perhaps he might wriggle through if he were careful.

With the first dead branch he had broken off, he lay and considered something that had just occurred to him. The stick was fairly tough, about the size of a walking stick. It had a crook at the tip. It had struck him that he might be able to work his rifle out of its scabbard and drag it up to where he could get hold of it. A risky business, especially if someone decided to ride down there and investigate. Cash Farley might even take a notion to have that saddle. There wasn't a better one in the country that Chip had seen, so far, and the one Cash had been riding the other day wasn't such great shakes. He might want to change before he went on.

But the carbine Chip couldn't bring himself to leave, if there was any possible way of getting it. He wriggled himself around and started back, dragging the stick carefully so that it would not break. Dead sage was pretty brittle . . .

There were no more shots, and that in itself worried Chip more than an occasional bullet would have done. He was afraid it meant that someone was coming down to make sure. It was not altogether the heat that made the sweat run down his face while he lay there fishing for that gun.

The stick was a little too large at the end. He had to bring it back and whittle it down, and that took time, in spite of his hurry. It was probably the only time in his life that Chip failed to do a neat job; and when he actually succeeded in working the gun out of its scabbard on to the ground he was so elated he forgot his caution and went after it with his hands. And for that indiscretion he felt a quick spiteful tug at his hat and knew, even before he heard, that a bullet had gone through it. The shot sounded closer too. Cash Farley was coming down.

On hands and knees, Chip scuttled to the bush, and close beside it he removed his hat and inched up until he could look out over the gully's brim. What he saw made him catch his breath, but he eased up the rifle, took aim and fired at the horseman picking his way down the steep coulee wall. Then he slid to the bottom, folded himself together and scuttled down the gully.

He was seen. Bullets followed him, a bullet nipped the point of his shoulder and made him jerk down under cover for a minute until he could better choose his line of retreat. He was near the end of this particular gully, where it merged with a wider, deeper ravine. But at the point of meeting it flattened, widened until there was no cover at all.

He had to risk it. He had to get back up on the bench if he could, back where Weary and Cal could be warned. He halted and lay against the sheltered bank, sighted along his rifle barrel, moving it slowly until it picked up a target; got it and fired. He could not wait to see whether he hit any one.

Over the lip of the deeper gulch he tripped and fell head-long, striking his knee against a rock with a force that numbed his whole leg for a minute. Afterwards he knew that fall must have saved his life, because when he picked up his hat, he saw where it had collected another bullet hole; two, to be exact; the small, brown-rimmed hole where the bullet struck, and the ragged tear where it went on through. But for the moment he was safe, hidden from sight beneath that three-foot drop.

Not so safe, either, for he heard the strident buzz of a rattlesnake among the rocks ten feet away, and his quick glance gave him a glimpse of a thick, mottled-gray body sliding into a slow coil. For the first time in his life he let a rattler go without making an effort to batter out its poisonous life. No time now—something worse than rattlesnakes had to be fought to a finish. Chip picked up his carbine, examined it anxiously to make sure it was not broken anywhere, felt to make sure his six-shooter had not dropped from his holster, moved that to a safer place inside his waistband in front, where he could better protect it, and hobbled off down the gulch.

This led straight to the creek bottom which offered plenty of cover and wound away for miles in either direction. An ideal place to dodge bullets. One that would keep several men busy for hours, hunting him out.

So he kept away from that creek bottom, dodging instead into the next gully that looked deep enough to hide him, and limping as fast as he could toward the low benchland, expecting to strike it north of the coulee. Let them hunt him down there in the brush. It would give him time to warn the boys, maybe.

He had reached the base of the steep hill and was looking for a way up that would not bring him into plain sight of any one below him, when a bullet spatted into a tuft of grass not six inches to one side of his shoulder.

So he had been seen again. With a sick feeling at the pit of his stomach, Chip made a crouching, scrambling run to a nest of boulders a few yards away. Wild currant bushes grew there, making a tangled screen into which he crashed as a leaden hornet stung his side. A rat darted out from under his body as he fell and a jack-rabbit bounced away up the hill. Bullets plopped into the hill behind him, snipping off fruit-laden branches as they zipped through the brush. More than once he heard the whining hum of a ricochet where a bullet had glanced from the rock.

They had him now, he realized with a dull resignation, when he had wriggled himself into a niche where he felt a trifle more secure. He could hold them off here for awhile—until they circled and came around behind him on the edge of the bluff. When that happened, he could see his finish. There was no possible way of protecting his back from the lead they could pour into it. Once they got above him, he told himself grimly, they'd have him dead to rights. He wouldn't even be able to make a run for it. They'd tumble him heels over head like a shot rabbit.

He'd fooled them for a few minutes, anyway. They had gone into the creek bottom looking for him—but they must have eyes like a hawk. Some one had seen him up against the hill. They'd start closing in now. That would give him a chance to get back at them, maybe. Good thing he'd filled up his cartridge belt that morning with one side all rifle shells. He ought to be able to do some damage before they got him. Pay for Dude's life, if nothing more.

With his carbine wedged between two rocks which gave sufficient play for aiming, Chip peered through a lower crevice, looking for horsemen down toward the creek. He did not see any, but he did catch the telltale glint of sunlight on metal, down about halfway and up near the top of the gulch. He lifted himself a little, drew a fine bead a few inches below the glitter and fired. Immediately he crouched down and looked through the crevice.

What he saw was a puff of smoke. An instant later a shiny black cluster of ripe currants dropped on his shoulder, slid down neatly into his hand. The finely ridged green leaves were moistly red, a phenomenon he could not account for until he put up his hand and felt the blood on his shoulder. "Hell!" he thought fiercely, "if it was bad, I guess I'd have found it out before now," and rose up and fired, taking careful aim at the rock where the blue flower of smoke had bloomed a few seconds ago. He could not tell what success he had, for the smoke still hung there, veiling any gun shine there might have been.

"Pung-ng-ng!" sang a bit of lead just above him, though no fresh blob of smoke down the gulch had warned him it was coming. That meant another gun somewhere off to the side, getting an angle that glanced a bullet off the rounded side of the boulder. *Zip-p-p* came another, off to the other side, flicking off leaves and twigs, as it tore through the bushes. They couldn't

see him, but they knew he was there and they were closing in on him.

Not too close, however. They had not silenced that 30-30 yet, and until they did, they were keeping at a respectful distance. In half an hour Chip was ringed round with men intent on killing him before they were done. Methodically, with a deadly patience that turned his blood to ice water, they were sending a cross-fire into that clump of brush. If they could not see the rocks, they must have guessed he had a natural barricade which they hoped by some lucky shot to penetrate, for they placed their bullets here and there, lacing the greenery with lines of death. And without wasting ammunition more than he must, he answered them with slugs able to end the argument, if they ever found the men they were looking for.

But they had him trapped, he knew that. Four rifles, so far, he knew were in action. There must be more. If they were riding around to come at him from the top . . .

It happened. From up on the hill the *pow-w* of a rifle floated down to him, sending a chill to the middle of his bones. He tried to crouch lower, looked wildly here and there for cover. There wasn't any. That first shot must have gone over; it wasn't easy to shoot straight down-hill and hit what you aimed at. But he was in plain sight—he had no way of hiding. They'd get the range and that would be the end.

"Hope he's a good shot," he muttered to himself, and shivered as if a cold wind had struck his bare flesh. That sounded like a 30-30, up there. Second time he'd missed. When he did hit, Chip hoped it would finish

226

him quick. The thought of a bullet plowing into his flesh, tearing muscles and tendons, smashing bones and yet not killing him was horrible. He didn't want them to get him alive —they might try some of those Injun tricks they had talked about that night he led them in to Cow Island; things they said they'd do to him when they caught him; things unthinkable.

He pulled his thoughts away from such horrors; away from the shooting as much as he could, except when he thought he saw a mark to aim at. He tried to think of Goldilocks, but those thoughts blurred like a reflection in water, when a breeze passes over the pool. Blue eyes and honey-colored hair—that was all he could see of her. And presently that too faded. He had to think of himself now. He had to think what he should do if they just shot him helpless. Trust to their mercy?

Answering that question, he pulled his six-gun from his belt and looked at it gravely, laid it down beside him where his hand would fall upon it easily. Unless they got him in the head or the heart—when it wouldn't matter—he'd have strength enough to lift that gun and pull the trigger, surely. After that, he felt better. He took the carbine, pulled cartridges from his belt, and slipped them one by one into the magazine; blew a bit of bark from the mechanism and settled himself to fight back. When they did come, damn them, they wouldn't find him with a lot of ammunition on hand.

Minutes crawled like snails. The guns out front had shifted position. They kept blazing away, but he couldn't see the smoke from where he was. Occasionally a bullet tore through the bushes or spatted against a rock, but it seemed as though those fellows up on the hill were a long time getting the range. They kept on shooting, but they hadn't come within a yard of him yet.

A man off to the right gave a squawking kind of screech as if he had been hit where it hurt—and Chip had not fired in that direction lately but to the left. The gun in front was silent. Down near the mouth of the gully a horseman galloped out of sight going toward the creek bottom. The shooting went on up there on the hill, but everywhere else was silent. Even the man who had been yelling out there yelled no more. And that was strange.

Then a voice came booming down from the hill-top. "Hey, Chip! Y' all right? Where'bouts is your horse?"

Weary! Good old Weary Willie up there, putting Cash Farley on the run! Chip clawed to his feet, waved a hand and tried to yell. To his surprise, no sound would come from his dry throat, and his darned legs wanted to fold up under him all the time. But it was all right—the boys were up there and they'd take charge of everything. Maybe it was his side that made him feel so kind of wobbly . . .

Funny, the way the boys got down there so darned quick. He had just sat down—or so it seemed to him—when here they were, milling around that clump of brush like a bunch of cattle around spilled blood. He wasn't sitting, however, he was lying on his back; and Weary was trying to take his shirt off in pieces, it looked like. Chip pushed away his hands and tried to get up.

228

"Lay still, 'fore I brain yuh! You're hurt, boy—yuh know that, or don't yuh?"

"Nicked a little, that's all. For outlaws, I will say that bunch is the poorest shots—" Chip didn't like the sound of his voice. It sounded as though it had been wrung dry; kind of weak and washed out. "I'm all right," he added gruffly. "Where did they go to?"

"Hell," Cal Emmett told him succinctly. "Where they belong."

"You mean—" Chip struggled to his feet and stood there weaving drunkenly, supported by Weary and Ted Culver. "Cash Farley?"

"Cash Farley," Cal nodded grimly. "Deader'n hell in a preacher's back yard. Shot three times, so I guess we'll have to draw straws on who collects the bounty on his pelt. And a couple of—"

"Say, I got Cash Farley, by golly," Slim spoke up in a boastful tone. "Drawed a bead on 'im and seen 'im keel over, by golly."

"You seen him keel over with my bullit in 'im then," Penny contended heatedly. "Want me to go pry it out of his guts and prove it to yuh? That old 30-30 of yourn couldn't hit the broad side of a barn."

"Hunh!" snorted Cal. "Don't go and lay that to the gun. It's Slim—"

"Where's your horse, Chip?" Weary interrupted the argument to ask. "Jar loose, you fellows. We've got to get him home."

"I'm all right, I tell yuh. I—they got Dude, but I want the saddle off him—straight out from the coulee . . ."

Weary caught him as he went down.

26. The How and the Why

UP IN THE PASTURE WHERE HE HAD GONE TO GET AWAY
from the endless wrangling of the Happy Family, Chip
was sitting with his back against a cottonwood tree,
smoking and trying to compose a letter to his
Goldilocks. It wasn't easy, though it had seemed simple
enough last night when he lay in bed thinking about it.
It wasn't supposed to be a love letter, yet he wanted it a
little different from the ordinary friendly note any
fellow would write. He wanted to send her the picture
he had made of her, and he wanted her to be sure and
get the secret meaning in the picture. He would not
come right out and tell her that Milt Cummings was the
snake and she had better look out for him; he wanted to
word the note so that Julie would read between the lines
and get his warning. A nice problem, that.

Then, without actually telling her so, he wanted to let
her know that he was busy planning their future
together, and that if he didn't see her very soon, it was
because he was getting right down to business and
making every day and every dollar count. And if he
could manage to mention the fact that he was keeping
an eye out for a good homestead, so that the minute he
was of age he could go ahead and file on it, she'd know
then just what his plans were. He didn't want to keep
her in the dark any longer than he had to. It didn't seem
right.

And there was another thing. He didn't want her to
think that he had brought on that fight with Big Butch's

men, or had killed Cash Farley or any one else. He might have, but the boys seemed to think they had done it all themselves. He wanted Goldilocks to know that all he did was defend himself, and that he was not the killer type and she needn't worry about his ever being that kind. And of course he ought to tell her that he wasn't hurt at all to speak of. A couple of bullet gashes that made him bleed like a stuck pig—he'd put it in nicer language than that, of course—so he was kind of knocked out for awhile and hadn't done much riding for a few days. His side was sore as a boil—but he wouldn't say anything about that, nor about his shoulder and knee.

All told, his hope was to condense about ten pages of love letter into a dozen lines that would carry his message and his undying love, yet which any stranger could read without calling him softer than hot mush. A full day's work for this mild Sabbath day, as any one would agree who knew what it was he was trying to do.

By noon he had written "Dear Goldilocks:" in beautiful Spencerian script, the D and the G nicely shaded, as was proper when you were writing a letter of such special significance. For a full half hour he had been sitting there, staring down at the words, wondering if it would sound too mushy if he wrote it "Dear Little Goldilocks" instead. He wanted to. Every word counted for a lot, and if he began with "Dear Little Goldilocks" he wouldn't have to say another word about how he felt toward her. She'd know. The devil of it was, so would any one else who might get hold of the letter.

Oh, well—hell, they'd know anyway that he must

231

like her a lot or he wouldn't he writing to her at all. Let them keep their damned noses out of other people's letters. It sure wouldn't be healthy for them if he ever found it out. So he folded down that sheet exactly on the line below the words, tore off the upper strip and rolled it into a tight little cylinder which he dropped into his coat pocket, along with the many tight little pills of cigarette paper that had accumulated there since the fight. And on a fresh sheet of paper he wrote "Dear Little Goldilocks" with a distinct quickening of the pulse in his writing wrist and a warm feeling in his face, though he sat in the shade. Which proves what power lies within a word.

Too much power. The longer he stared at it, the mushier it looked. And after awhile he tore that off as he had the other, and reduced it to bits the size of a child's finger nail, making sure that no two letters remained on one fragment. Then he hunted the other wad out of his pocket and tore that up also. He had suddenly found himself completely out of the notion of writing any letter at all. Hell, he'd be seeing her one of these days. He guessed all he had to say would keep.

A stir among his horses that had been contentedly feeding around him lifted his eyes and his thoughts from the paper before him. Rummy and little Silver were starting for the fence, taking two or three tentative steps and then stopping to start again. Silvia moved after them, then decided she wouldn't bother. It was only Weary Willie coming, and the colts would follow him back. Mike deigned only one long glance at the cowboy stilting along on his high heels. Mike knew that one; he switched a fly off his rump, blew flower pollen from his nostrils and moved off—not that he expected to be wanted, but just in case.

"Hey, Chip! Y'ain't tryin' to break yourself of the habit of eatin', are yuh? Dinner's about ready, I guess. I saw Patsy puttin' dumplin's into a kettle of them grouse Slim brought in—and if I was you, I'd kinda edge up towards the feed trough. Six grouse are sure going to last quick when them yahoos land at the table." Weary made a pass at Rummy, meaning to grab him by the mane, and grinned foolishly when the colt was not there at all. "Mamma, he's quick! Well, come on. What yuh been doin' with yourself all morning?"

"Nothing." Chip lifted himself up as carefully as an old man, slipping the tablet into his coat pocket.

"How's the knee and the side and all the rest of yuh?"

"All right. Knee's stiff as the devil; got a kink in it somewhere, I guess. You, Rummy! You bite Silver once more and I'll brain yuh with a rock!" Chip grinned as he turned away to limp through the gate Weary had opened for him. "Talk about the devil entering into a drove of hogs—if there ain't seven devils in that damned colt, I miss my guess."

"Sure is a corker, all right. If he keeps on the way he's started, he sure will be a rim-runner, one of these days, now I'm tellin' yuh." He looked at Chip with a twinkle in his eyes. "What's the chance of tradin' yuh out of that colt?"

"You go to hell," Chip advised him sweetly.

A new covered buggy, shiny black where the dust of the trail had not dimmed its luster, had just turned out of the creek bottom below the corrals and was coming toward the camp. "Now who the devil is that?" ejaculated Weary. "Milt's brown team—but he always drove a buckboard. Mamma! He's gettin' up in the world, stakin' himself to a new top buggy. . . . Wonder—"

Weary did not finish that sentence. He knew who sat on the seat beside Milt Cummings. He wondered if Chip knew, but he tactfully refrained from asking.

Chip did know. By the thump of his heart he knew it before Weary did. It was Goldilocks, coming to see him. Wanting to see him so much that she got Milt to bring her. He wished she hadn't—wished she wouldn't put herself under obligations to Milt Cummings, even though it did show how much she cared.

By the time the two reached the cabins, the team had pulled in and stopped. Milt was out, helping Julie down—holding her closer and longer than he'd any business to, Chip thought with fury. And she didn't seem to give a darn! Just laughed and blushed like . . .

"Folks, meet Mrs. Cummings!" Milt's exultant voice halted Chip's thoughts and left his brain absolutely blank. "Kinda slipped one over on you, didn't we? Pretty cute at dodgin' the loop, but I sure got her noosed now—for keeps."

Cal Emmett, with what Chip mentally termed the gall of a brass monkey, saved the situation by bellowing, "And I'm sure goin' t' kiss the bride!" Which he proceeded to do, while Milt stood back and pretended to pull his gun.

In the mêlée that followed—most of the boys claiming the privilege Cal had taken—Chip achieved a certain degree of calmness which he hoped would convince that blue-eyed little Jezebel how little he cared. It was his most aloof, most coldly condescending manner, had he only known it. It gave the effect of a young man with a chip on his shoulder (meaning no pun whatever). It wouldn't have deceived a soul that took time to notice him. But no one did, because Patsy whanged the dishpan just then and J.G. came hobbling out of his cabin, supported by Slim and Shorty, which was a second huge surprise to the Happy Family. Then, of course, there were the six grouse and dumplings, made to go farther by the addition of a couple of cottontails one of the boys had shot that morning. Ted Culver and Happy Jack took the team and a led horse down to the corral and legged it back, so they wouldn't miss anything, and babel filled the mess house for an hour. Chip had plenty of time to compose himself.

It was not until dinner was over that he and Milt exchanged any speech, or that Julie gave him more than a fleeting glance. Milt crooked a finger at him and started for the buggy, Julie walking beside him with her two hands clasped around his arm. Chip came near limping off in the opposite direction, but there had been something very definite in that gesture. He thought maybe those two were going to try and explain or something, and if so, he'd sure see that they got no satisfaction out of him.

Milt went around to the roomy box behind the seat. As he reached in to pull out a bag of something, he looked up at Chip, his eyes showing green, as the sun shone in them. "Julie said you wanted your brother's stuff, so I thought I'd bring it over," he said. "It's all here but his spurs—I—he had them on—that night."

Chip swallowed dryly, leaned hard against the wheel. "I—thanks," he said huskily. It was all he could think of to say.

Milt tilted his bare head toward the corral. "I brought his other horse—Pegleg, he called him. He's down there in the corral. This is the bed and his clothes and— well, you know. Odds and ends; trinkets he had. You got his saddle horse and riding outfit away from Cash Farley, so I guess this covers it all."

"You poor boy," Julie said softly, and laid her hand with its new rings on his shoulder. "We're just as sorry as we can be—"

"Thanks." Chip moved so that her hand slid down away from him. He looked at Milt. "How did Cash Farley get hold of that horse and saddle?"

"Stole 'em. Wane was riding along in the edge of the hill one day last fall—just a week or so before he was killed—"

"Killed?"

"Yeah. I didn't know this till just the other day. I got it out of one of Cash Farley's cronies. I knew how he lost the horse, of course. It was along toward evening. He was going over to Lang's—to see Julie. She'd spoke about making chokecherry jell, and Wane knew where there was some dandies, so he rode over there with a flour sack to get her some."

"He did, too. Great big ones, just lovely—" Julie interpolated, clasping Milt's arm again.

"Yeah. Well, he was pickin' along and never heard a thing outa the way, but when he went to get on his horse, it was gone. He'd went off quite a piece, he said; farther than he thought at the time. You know how it is when you get interested, and the patch was kinda scattered up along a gully—Well, anyway, he had to walk home and catch up another horse, and he never did find out what became of his sorrel.

"Not till that last night. He'd hunted and asked everybody around over this way, I guess. I was busy and never paid much attention at the time. Just s'posed the horse had strayed off.

"Well, this feller I was talkin' to—he was afraid to say anything while Cash was alive; Cash was a bad actor all right. It was him give Butch most of his bad name. Butch ain't as bad as folks try to make out. He wasn't in on this fight you had—didn't know what Cash was pullin'—

"Well, Wane had been to Lang's that night and was just goin' home—pretty late, huh, Julie?"

"No later than you used to stay, silly!"

"Anyway, as he was crossin' the river, here come Cash Farley ridin' the sorrel. Cash told about it afterwards, to this feller that told me yesterday. Wane hollered to him to get off that horse and made a play for his gun. And Cash beat him to it—shot him off his horse and turned around and rode back to camp. He said Wane hung onto the reins and pulled the horse off into swimmin' water." Milt stopped, drew a long breath. "It's hell, kid. Nobody ever thought more of Wane Bennett than I did; as a friend, I mean. But he didn't suffer any. And he went out fightin'—and I guess that's as good a way as any.

"Anyway, Cash Farley was the man that done it, and you got him; or some of your outfit did. You got that much satisfaction. Cash didn't get away with it long."

He pulled out the thin bed roll and a warbag that wrenched Chip's heart to look at. It had W.B. and the brand B on the side. Chip had put them there the night before Wane rode north. He ground his teeth together, reached out and took the bag from Milt.

"Where yuh want this bed roll? In the bunk house? I'll carry it in for yuh."

In the shade the Happy Family were roosting, talking in low tones together as they smoked, careful not to seem to know what was going on at the buggy. Weary and Cal edged over to make a passage to the bunk house door. Milt went in, stood the roll against the wall, turned and grasped Chip's hand. "I throwed it into yuh kinda hard when you first come," he said. "I was a plumb crazy fool over Julie. I know now there was nothin' between you two. I'd like to be friends."

"Thanks."

"And I want yuh to know I and Wane thought a lot of each other. I'm sorry as hell about everything."

"Thanks."

Milt clamped his fingers on Chip's uninjured shoulder, turned and went out. Chip closed the door after him, kicked a box against it.

The Happy Family took the hint. Slowly, one by one, so as to make it seem casual, they got up and drifted off down to the corral, Milt and Julie following slowly, arm in arm. In the bunk house Chip sat on the side of his bunk, staring at that warbag and the letters neatly painted upon it. And his thoughts were not of any person called Goldilocks. They were back in Denver two years ago, when he was telling Wane good-by.

Center Point Publishing
600 Brooks Road • PO Box 1
Thorndike ME 04986-0001 USA

(207) 568-3717

US & Canada:
1 800 929-9108